ANGEL FAE

THE WORLD OF FAE, BOOK 11

TERRY SPEAR

WILDE INK PUBLISHING

PUBLISHED BY:

Wilde Ink Publishing
    Angel Fae
    Copyright © 2021 by Terry Spear
    Cover Copyright by Ravven

Discover more about Terry Spear at:
    http://www.terryspear.com/

Print ISBN: 978-1-63311-079-3
    Ebook ISBN: 978-1-63311-078-6

FOREWORD

Synopsis

Hawk fae Ariana is a guard for the royal family, a highly coveted position, and one she has worked hard at, but in one trip to the human world to have fun in the sun with her friend, she makes the mistake of saving a couple of children from drowning in the Gulf of Mexico. Now she's living in a new world with the Angel Corp in the angel realm of existence, and she's required to save both humans and fae alike. Before she has gotten her feet wet on the easier assignments, she's stuck with the really dangerous stuff. But she can't die, can she? She has already done that once. But she wants to return to the fae world—the living fae world—in any way that she can.

Malik was supposed to have been Ariana's guardian angel but when he saw another human struggling in the riptide, he went to save him, thinking that Ariana was going to be just fine. Now he is her mentor in the Angel Corp, when he'd always wanted to get to know her better while they'd both been of the fae world. This situation of her wanting to return as a fae is a deadly business.

But if she manages to do so safely, she'll leave him behind. Now she's working on all dangerous missions and he's afraid he'll lose her for good. Still, helping her to return to the fae world of the living isn't in the plans.

Dedicated to Jac Broin who gave me a whole list of fae characters she wants to see more of! Thanks, Jac. I'm so glad you're loving them. And yes!! I need to finish up the Magic of Inherian series also!

PROLOGUE

As a guard for the hawk fae royal family, Ariana was riding horseback near King Tiernan while he was hunting with a party of fifteen men and women in Shadow Wood Forest in his kingdom. Ariana and four other royal guards, one of whom was her best friend Charity, were keeping an eye on the king to protect him, watching for any danger that might suddenly present itself. King Tiernan really didn't like having the guards follow him when he was hunting with his bow, afraid that he might miss taking down the wild boar if his guards accidentally scared off his prey. But she took her job seriously, and letting the king hunt by himself, wasn't something she or any of the royal guards would agree to. In the meantime, other royal guards were still back at the castle, watching over his wife, Queen Ritasia, and his sister, Princess Esmeralda.

Normally, Ariana always was focused on the royals when they were beyond the castle walls, and inside also, in case an assassin tried to attempt to kill the king or his wife or sister when they were at home. But this time, Ariana was thinking of her boyfriend, Claude, and how he wanted to be part of the king's royal guards so badly, she wondered sometimes if that was why he had befriended her and begun to date her. Even if he wasn't selected for the royal guard staff, maybe he felt he had sort of an in that way.

Charity kept warning Ariana the fae was no good. That when he wasn't in Ariana's sights, he was mixing it up with single females when he should have been loyal to Ariana. Sure, it bothered her, but she wasn't interested in anyone else to date at the moment, so she figured she'd play along for now. Though if *she* caught him sneaking around with another fae, that was another story.

The hunters suddenly were shouting they'd spotted a wild boar north of the king's location and he and the rest of the men and women took off to hunt the boar down for dinner. She and the royal guards raced to keep up with them when she saw a dark-haired fae carrying a readied bow in the woods running, and then aiming an arrow at the king. An assassin!

The fae was hiding his aura so she couldn't tell which kind he was. He was concentrating so hard on the king that he didn't even notice she was close enough to him that she could leap from her horse from behind and take him down. She dove for him and slammed into him, knocking him to the ground, both of them landing hard. She planned to lock him in iron manacles to keep him from fae transporting out of there so the king could decide his fate, but the assassin struck her hard in the head with his balled-up fist, momentarily stunning her. Despite that, she managed to grab his bow away from him and held on tight so he couldn't jerk it out of her grasp and have another attempt at the king's life. The dark-eyed and haired assassin scowled at her and vanished.

Rolling onto her back, she lay on the ground in the woods, still grasping the assassin's crimson bow. She realized then that everyone was gone—the hunters, the king, the other royal guards, the assassin. Even her horse had run off to be with the rest of them and her head was pounding, but at least she had the assassin's bow in hand, if anyone should think she just fell off her horse. Dazed, she sat up and finally managed to stand, using the trunk of a tree to steady herself. Then she looked for the arrow that the assassin had released and found it in a tree near where the king had been just moments earlier. Thankfully, when she had jumped on the fae, she'd thrown him off balance and his arrow missed its target.

She heard the men cheering off in the distance and knew they'd taken down the boar. No one seemed to notice she was missing until her friend Charity shouted, "Ariana!"

Charity knew Ariana wouldn't abandon the king on the hunt without good reason. Maybe she'd seen Ariana's horse too without a rider.

Ariana's head was splitting in two. She would have transported to the location where the hunting party was otherwise, but she couldn't concentrate, seething still that she hadn't been able to take the assassin into custody.

"Here!" she called out, but her voice was unusually weak. Some guard she made about now. If anyone else threatened the king's life, she wouldn't be able to do anything about it. "Stay with the king!" That was Charity's job right now. Not to take care of Ariana. She would live.

Two of the hunters returned for her with her horse in tow—the traitor—and she pointed to the assassin's arrow embedded in the tree.

"An assassin?" one of the men asked, his eyes wide with shock. Nobody had suspected it and she figured the assassin had left, not attempting to make another attempt on the king's life. It was too late for that.

"Yeah, and he got away. But not without this." She held up his bow and then she slid to the ground, her vision slipping into darkness.

* * *

As a royal guard and phantom fae, Malik had time off and he returned to South Padre Island, his favorite place to visit in the human world, even though this was dark fae claimed territory. But through peace treaties, his people were at peace with the dark fae…for now. That was always subject to change. But what really brought him here whenever he was free from work was trying to see the object of his desire—a hawk fae by the name of Ariana, hoping she'd be there. He'd never actually talked to her when he'd seen her here before, though he'd been dying to. He just hadn't gotten up the nerve yet.

He was on a boat in the Gulf of Mexico, the human men in it fishing. He was invisible to them, though if he'd wanted to pull a prank on them, he would just appear and scare them to pieces, but he was too interested in watching for Ariana. Then she suddenly appeared with her friend Charity on the white sand beach, Ariana's head bandaged, a bloody area on the side of it. He wanted to take whoever had hurt Ariana to task, if someone had.

Her white, blond hair was whipping around her in the breeze, and she was wearing a pretty pink bathing suit and a sheer, scarf-like skirt over that, tied at the waist. She was so otherworldly in a beautiful and mystical way, he couldn't deny his attraction to her.

He couldn't hear them, but he could read lips and he was "listening" to their conversation.

"You saved the king, and this is part of his repayment, especially since you were injured. I'm here to see that you enjoy yourself," Charity said. "And don't come to any other harm, you know, since you kept the assassin's bow."

"I didn't *catch* the assassin," Ariana said. "He got away."

Charity patted her on her shoulder. "You got his weapon. You stopped him from harming the king. The assassin nearly killed you. You did the best you could do." Then Charity spied a blond male flexing his muscles in front of a couple of females. "Oh, there's a human I want to mess with. Have fun. That's what the royal family wants you to do—is just to have a good time."

If Malik could, he would take down the assassin himself for hurting Ariana.

Malik wished he could just go up to her and talk to her, but what if she turned him down? He swore he'd built this all up in his mind about getting to know her. She might not be interested in meeting him at all. He was a phantom fae, not a hawk fae, and not all fae liked to mix it up.

The men in the fishing boat began moving about in it, rocking it. He knew the disaster that could be if they didn't settle down, but he was concentrating on Ariana so hard that he wasn't paying enough attention to the men. The next thing he knew, the boat began to tip precariously in the rough surf. He planned to transport to the beach after the men had ended up in the water and he saved them. But before he could save himself, the boat tipped hard, smacked him in the head, and knocked him out.

That was the end of his life as he'd known it. He should have gone to speak with Ariana on the beach like he'd desperately wanted to instead.

CHAPTER 1

Queen Ritasia had given Ariana a few days off after being injured while saving the king for the fifth time this year. Though she'd only been injured like this twice, and Ariana had taken down the assassins for good all the rest of the times but that one. She still held onto the assassin's crimson bow in case he thought to return for it.

Charity was given the job of watching out for Ariana and ensuring she had a good time—again. The royal family hadn't allowed Ariana to serve as a royal guard since being injured while the king and his entourage were traveling to another kingdom and that was driving her crazy.

Like other fae, Ariana had gone to the human world to mingle with humans, the faes' favorite pastime. Infiltrate them, play tricks on them, it was the fae way. Though she had to admit, she hadn't wanted to play with the humans.

Charity said, "Come on. It will do you good to just have some fun. We're constantly guarding the royal family, making sure they stay safe. You deserve this. You need the break from reality and to rest up."

When they arrived at their favorite spot—South Padre Island

TERRY SPEAR

—they discovered that storms had swept through the area, and waves were capping in the Gulf of Mexico. Normally when they visited here the water was fairly calm.

"Riptide warnings," Charity said. "Oh, and look at all the foolish humans swimming in the surf because of the cool waves. Hey, and forget about Claude. He doesn't deserve you. You're lucky to be rid of him."

Yeah, Ariana had dumped Claude because she'd finally caught him with another fae, but she didn't care. She should have been feeling hurt or angry, but all she cared about was losing her grandmother a few weeks ago, who had been like a mother to her after Ariana's own mother had perished at sea in a boating accident five years earlier.

Charity sighed. "You've got to look at the bright side of things. We're here." She spread her arms out wide. "The storm has passed, and the sun is trying to come out. The weather is beautiful. And oh, I see a stunning guy I want to talk to."

Ariana took a deep breath. Even the white sand beaches and windswept water held no appeal for her. She should have just gone home. She really didn't feel like messing with humans today.

"Coming?" Charity asked.

"No. Go have fun. I'm going to watch the humans playing in the surf." Ariana felt disquieted. She shouldn't have cared about the humans, or their safety. She was fae and it wasn't normal to feel things like that. But she couldn't help but worry about the ones who were putting themselves at risk in the tugging currents. Maybe her abnormal feelings were because she had worried her grandmother was going to die and then nothing could save her. Or maybe because her mother had died at sea under similar conditions.

Ariana glanced at Charity and saw her flirting with a blond-haired guy, twisting her dark hair around her finger in a coy way. She was good at getting their attention and then when she had

8

them hooked, she would vanish, making them think they'd witnessed a ghost.

A kid screamed in the water and Ariana's heart stuttered as she swiftly shifted her gaze to the Gulf. Three girls, about ten years of age, were playing in the surf—two redheads and a black-haired girl.

"Not safe for them, is it?" A guy asked near her and her heart about gave out.

She turned to see a guy as dark haired as Charity standing near her, his dark brown eyes focused on the swimmers, his arms folded across his chest. He was wearing black board shorts featuring a killer whale. Her own bathing suit was a one-piece light pink. That was her signature color when she wasn't working and wearing the royal blue and gold armor as a royal guard. Pastel pinks, blues, and teals. She liked soft and sheer, not frilly, but silky, flowing, and so she was wearing a wraparound skirt of filmy pink gauze and strappy white sandals.

She didn't recognize the fae, and she realized he was hiding his fae aura, which reminded her of the assassin fae she'd taken down but lost. Why hide his fae aura unless he was up to no good?

She didn't answer him, not wanting to socialize with him.

"My name is Malik. And you are?"

She sighed. "Ariana, a hawk fae."

He smiled. "It's good to meet you."

She wasn't sure why she told him she was a hawk fae. He could see that's what she was.

"Why are you watching the swimmers? Why not swim?" he asked, folding his arms, not taking a hint that she didn't want to visit with him.

She ignored him. Go away, she wanted to tell him. Then she let out her breath and glanced at him. He was still watching the swimmers, not looking at her as if she really didn't exist and he was just bored and talking out loud to himself. He was really hot, if he hadn't been an aura-less fae.

"Why aren't *you* swimming?" she finally asked.

"It's too dangerous."

"You could just"—she waved her hand—"vanish if things get too perilous for you."

"So could you."

But she didn't want to swim. She was only here because her friend wanted her to come with her. Sure, she was dressed for the beach. That was it. No sense in wearing human jeans to the beach when a swimsuit suited the setting better, but it didn't mean she wanted to swim or sunbathe or flirt with a human *or* a fae.

The Gulf breeze whipped her long blond hair about, and it slapped his shoulder. But he didn't move away from her.

He turned his dark-eyed gaze on her, looking as serious as could be, and said, "I'm here to save you."

She raised her brows. "Really?" That had to be a guy line if she ever heard one.

"Yeah." He watched the swimmers again.

"Well, you're wasting your time. I don't need you to save me." Then she wondered if he was psychic or something. She knew some fae were, though she hadn't known any personally. But it made her wonder if he knew something she didn't. "You're psychic?"

He smiled. "Hardly."

She shook her head and thought to return home, but she didn't want to abandon Charity if she got *herself* into trouble. Then Ariana heard another kid's scream and she glanced at the three girls she'd been watching. One of the redheaded girls had gone under the water. Maybe just a wave had crested and buried her. Ariana assumed the child would come back up for air. But she didn't. And Ariana did something so uncharacteristic for their kind, that she wasn't even sure why she had done it. She dove into the water to save the child. She came up for air and saw another child being swept away.

No! No! No!

Where were the humans who should have been watching their kids? Or anyone, really? Lifeguards? Rescue swimmers? The Coast Guard?

Ariana couldn't find the child she'd gone after. Then she came up for air and saw the third child screaming, fighting for air. Ariana couldn't let them drown. The fae didn't save humans. That was the humans' business—they needed to take care of their own. Yet Ariana didn't stop searching for the child with the red hair and found her, pulling her out of the water, carrying her the rest of the way, and leaving her on the beach for her parents to take care of. They came running to see to her, paramedics rushing to the scene. *Finally.*

Then Ariana vanished, maybe to their astonishment unless they were too busy working on the little girl to save her life. Probably that was the case. She didn't care. All she could do was go after another one of the children, the darkhaired girl. That's when she saw the aura-less fae, Malik, who had been standing next to her earlier, bringing in the other redheaded child. She was grateful he had helped with one of the kids.

The riptide was pulling the darkhaired girl way out to the Gulf. She disappeared behind high waves and Ariana appeared next to the panicking girl in the fae way, faster to travel that way than trying to swim through the rough surf like a human would have to.

Ariana dove for the little girl in the trough between waves. Both of them were dunked and she and the girl came up coughing. Ariana thought she saw Malik dive in to save another person who had been dragged out by the riptide, a man. Ariana finally found the girl and held onto her to keep her head above water, though the girl was terrified and screaming.

Ariana had choked on so much salty water herself, she

couldn't even focus on transporting the girl to the shore like she'd done with the other. Then she saw a boat had been launched and was coming for them. Ariana was trying to keep the girl afloat in the big waves, way out in the Gulf, hoping they would reach her in time. The girl kept pushing Ariana under the water and Ariana was having a devil of a time catching her breath or keeping the girl from drowning.

Suddenly the girl was lifted out of the water and into the boat and Ariana went under for the final time.

* * *

MALIK KNEW he'd made a *big* mistake in trying to save the adult male human. Malik was supposed to be there for the hawk fae, Ariana. And he hadn't been. And she had drowned. Now, she was just like him. A guardian angel fae serving in the Angel Corp, having to prevent fae, or humans, from dying.

He should have saved her. The man he'd tried to save had drowned anyway. But Malik's focus was supposed to have been solely on Ariana—no one else. He'd managed to save the one little girl and Ariana had saved the other two and he thought Ariana looked relieved that he'd done that much. Which had been in his noble reason for doing so. To impress her.

When he saw Ariana again, he suspected she wouldn't be happy with him, even though the first time he'd ever seen her at the beach with her friend, he'd wanted to get to know Ariana a whole lot better.

This hadn't been the way he'd meant to do it though.

CHAPTER 2

When Ariana woke, she found herself in a white room, lying in a twin-size bed covered in white from the pillows and comforter to the bed skirt. She was wearing silky white pajamas that didn't belong to her. The walls in the room featured large, white framed pictures of—she frowned at the pictures—and realized they were *angels*? She closed her eyes and opened them again to peer at them. Angels. Big, white, feathery wings. Yep. Not the winged fae. Angels.

She thought she was in a human hospital room, but it didn't make any sense. She could have been pulled into the boat like she thought the little girl had been before she went under the waves for the final time after having swallowed so much water. But it hadn't been the final time, because someone had to have pulled her out of the Gulf and resuscitated her. She was here, wasn't she? Wherever *here* was.

A girl who appeared to be about Ariana's age whipped into the room, her black hair cut in a short bob, her dark eyes sparkling with excitement, and she smiled brightly at her. "Rise and shine. Time to meet your new boss, Catriona. I'm Juno. And you're Ariana."

"I work for the hawk king and queen. I'm part of the royal guard." Ariana frowned at the girl, dressed in a flowing lavender gown. She was hiding her fae aura also. What was up with that?

Where in the world was Ariana?

"No longer," the girl said cheerily. "You have a new job, but Catriona will tell you about it."

"No." Ariana was afraid she had made a big mistake in saving the two human girls, that she was in trouble for that and for vanishing and reappearing when they were supposed to be careful of that. In front of a human or two, was one thing. But a whole beach of people, that was another story.

Didn't she have any say in what she was supposed to work at? And why wouldn't she be working for the hawk fae king? Unless the king had fired her for vanishing while saving humans. Still, no way would she be working for some other fae without her knowledge.

Then Malik came into the room, and she was so surprised to see him there, she was momentarily at a loss for words. He was wearing blue jeans, sneakers, and a T-shirt that said: I Paused My Game to Be Here.

She frowned at him. "What are you doing here? And where am I?"

"I'm here to apologize to you. I was supposed to save you."

An odd sense of dread swept through her as she recalled their earlier conversation. But then she scoffed. "You saved one of the girls instead? No biggy. I'm here, aren't I?"

"Kind of."

She frowned at him.

"You're no longer with the royal guard for the hawk fae king and queen. You're one of us now. Part of the Angel Corp. Sorry. It's my fault. I went to save a human male, thinking the people in the boat who had pulled the other girl inside it after you kept her from drowning, had rescued you, but they hadn't. I've been read the riot act, of course. My job was to save you, and I lost you."

"Okay, I'm going to speak to the hawk fae king." Ariana meant to just vanish and reappear in the hawk fae kingdom, but nothing happened. That would only happen if she'd been confined in iron for some infraction of a rule, which took away a fae's ability to transport. She glanced at her wrists and ankles, as if she just hadn't realized she was wearing iron manacles, but she wasn't.

"You can't fae transport until Catriona tells you what you need to know and gives you your first assignment or two or three. Whenever she believes you've earned your right to fae travel again, you'll get your ability back."

"No way. This is all some kind of a practical joke. Or I'm having a bizarre nightmare." Ariana couldn't believe any of this was real.

Malik sighed. "We are angels—guardian angels, members of a combined fae of the Angel Corp where none of us are at war with one another."

"Okay, then, where are our wings? Your wings? Juno's wings?" Ariana waved at the pictures on the wall. "They all have wings. Don't tell me we have to earn them by saving someone." She didn't believe it for a minute. Last time she checked, it was summer, the month of July, not April Fool's Day, a favorite of the fae who had initially created it.

"Nope. That's a notion in the human world. You have them. I have them. Juno has them. Even Catriona has them. But we can choose to reveal them or not." One minute, Malik was standing there perfectly wingless, and the next minute, he was wearing huge, feathery white wings. Very becoming, she thought, in an angelic sort of way.

Ariana blinked, thinking to clear her vision. But nope, he was still standing there, wings folded behind his back. As if he thought he wasn't getting his point across to her, he spread them, flapped them even, sending a breeze in her direction, ruffling her clothes and hair. She felt as though she were standing on the beach in South Padre Island while the Gulf breezes swept around her.

Then she glanced at Juno. Maybe, Malik could play mind tricks on her. Some fae were known to be able to. Was Juno able to produce wings too?

Juno smiled and waved her arm as if she needed the extra showmanship. With a flourish, wings appeared behind her also. Beautiful white, feathery wings. She wrapped them around herself as if she were wearing a warm, winter cape of white feathers, a new part of her attire.

Then Juno unfolded them and flapped them like a butterfly, in, out, gently fluttering.

Ariana had to admit she was impressed, but she still didn't believe she could have wings since just thinking about unfurling them didn't make them appear for her. "Okay, so how do I produce the wings?"

"You have to speak with Catriona first. She'll set your wings free, after she tells you the rules and she decides you're ready for them," Malik said. "It's different for everyone."

Ariana didn't believe any of this. "How long have you been here, Juno?"

"I've been at this for two years. You have to speak with the angel in charge of newly turned angels in the Angel Corp," Juno said.

"Wait. I'm a hawk fae. What kind are you, Malik?" Ariana asked.

"Phantom fae." Malik bowed low.

"And you are?" Ariana asked Juno.

"Scorpion fae."

"All right, let's do this," Ariana said, still not believing this. She was having a night terror she couldn't wake up from for sure. But she noticed her fae aura was gone, and that didn't make any sense, unless she was having a nightmare.

"Malik will take you. He has been assigned as your mentor."

Juno smiled. "I just dropped in first to say hi. I've got other chores to perform, fae to save, or I might have to save a human today. Not sure. See you around." Juno vanished.

Malik smiled. "It will be my pleasure. But"—he motioned to Ariana's nightwear—"you might want to change your clothes first."

* * *

MALIK SUSPECTED Ariana would be a hard case, much like he had been when he had first arrived here, come to think of it. He wasn't sure she would be able to go on an assignment for a while, not until she learned to obey the rules. Like he hadn't been able to. He wondered if she would try to break out of the place, like he'd tried to do. And return to the world he'd known before this. He wanted to tell Ariana that if she did what Catriona told her to do, and she did it right, she might even be able to return to their fae world—and leave the Angel Corp as a living, breathing fae. Not that they didn't live and breathe here as angels, but it was just on a different plane of existence.

Catriona would want Ariana to start working on lots of missions soon, just like all the new guardian angels did, and see how well they handled their assignments, which would decide her life from then on.

Once Ariana left her room dressed in white shorts and a white and gold embossed tunic, she joined him. Her long, white-blond hair was braided with gold and crystals making her appear just as ethereal as he thought angels would look before he knew they came in all shapes and sizes and colorations and all different kinds of fae.

He led her down the white marble corridors, the soles of their leather shoes whisper soft so they didn't disturb anyone else in the hallowed halls.

"What did you do to get here?" Ariana asked.

17

"I was in a boat on the Gulf, watching people on the shore."

"Humans? Wanting to cause mischief among them?" she asked.

"Not exactly." He felt his face flush a little with heat. He couldn't help that he was embarrassed that he had been so infatuated with her.

She frowned. "What then?"

He only smiled, not wanting to tell her why he'd been on South Padre Island so much. He'd been watching for her, afraid she might think he'd been stalking her. But from the first time he'd first seen her on the beach with her friend three years ago, he'd wanted to meet her, despite that she had been a hawk fae.

"So how did you end up here?"

"Out of nowhere, a rogue wave capsized the boat. I was eaten by a shark."

She furrowed her brow at him, appearing to partly believe him.

He smiled. "It's a better story than saying the humans in the boat couldn't see me, of course, and they were moving about in it, not keeping low, unbalanced the boat, and capsized us. I was about to just transport out of there, but a sudden swell of a wave shoved the boat into me and hit me so hard on the head, it knocked me out, and I…drowned. In retrospect, I should have stayed on shore." To meet Ariana and he should have just built up the courage to talk to her. Though he hadn't wished for her to drown also, he was glad he could be with her here.

Not that he could do anything about it, despite that his intense infatuation of her hadn't dissipated once he had become an angel and now that she was one.

"I'm sorry that happened to you. What were you watching on the beach that held such fascination for you?"

Another man about their age came toward them, no wings, but he suddenly sprouted them and waved them, smiling brightly at Ariana, as he hurried on past.

Malik was annoyed.

"What was that all about? An angel greeting?" she asked.

"An angel showing interest in a new angel fae."

She rolled her eyes. "So how do you get out of this nightmare?"

He knew she would feel that way. Not all newly turned angels did. Some felt proud or distinguished, that they had more purpose in death than they'd had when they were alive. Others, like him, had wanted to reverse this "condition" and return to the way it was. He knew some had. Very few. And he wondered how they had fared. Did they return to their homes? Their people? Did anyone believe that they had been an angel for a time?

Did they even remember having been an angel at all? He wondered if they had retained their identity or when they had returned to the fae world, they had become someone else with a new identity completely. New memories. A whole new life.

He was certain Ariana would feel the same way as him.

"You need to be here for a while to see how you like it. See if you fit in. Some love it here. They love it more than where they were before in life."

"And you?"

He gave her a wry smile.

"You want to leave."

He wasn't sure. Not now that Ariana was here. Could he get to know her better? Finally? But angels didn't date. So he wasn't sure if anything could come of a relationship with her—other than just a friendship. Yet, he still wanted more. What was up with that anyway?

"I'm still trying to find my way." That's all he would say to her because he figured she would want to know what he knew about those who had returned to the fae world. Maybe they had to have learned some new life lessons, in a guardian angel sort of way first. How was he to know? All he knew was he had to take her to see Catriona and figure it out from there.

* * *

ARIANA COULDN'T BELIEVE the weird situation she was in. Sure, everyone had heard about guardian angels—mostly in the human world. In the fae world? She'd heard some rumors and of course her father's stories, but she really hadn't believed in any of it.

Ariana let out her breath, wondering if the stories her father had told her when she was younger *had* been true. "So one time, my father said a guardian angel had saved his life when he was a boy. An avalanche had swept down a mountain when he was hassling a group of skiers in the human world, and he was buried by the swiftly traveling snow. Wrong place at the wrong time kind of situation and he hadn't reacted quickly enough before he was buried. Of course, he was still alive after that, but he said it was because his guardian angel had been watching over him and led the rescue crew right to where he was and saved him. He could have just vanished, but he'd been so disoriented, he couldn't. A fae boy was with the rescue crew of humans. The fae my father hadn't known told him he was his guardian angel. He wasn't wearing wings or anything. Then once my father was rescued, the boy vanished."

"The boy might have been a guardian angel. Who else would call himself that if it wasn't so?" Malik said.

Ariana shrugged. "It's just a saying. You know that. Someone saves someone, just a fae, or human, consequence of being there at the right time, and voila, that person who would have died sees the person as their hero or guardian angel."

"Okay, that might be true. But you still feel that way even after learning about us?" Malik asked.

"I don't know about you yet."

He smiled. "I mean about what we are. That we have wings."

"I don't have any." She sighed. "So my dad said when he was younger, his mother ran over him with her horse. She didn't kill him, but he got lucky because the horse was distracted and ran clear over him, missing trampling him by inches."

"Your mother wanted to kill her son?" Malik appeared astounded to hear the news.

"No, of course not. She hadn't seen him. Anyway, he was okay, bruised, dirty, clothes torn, but there was a boy standing nearby who smiled at him and said he was his guardian angel. That time he had shown his wings."

"No." Malik sounded like he didn't believe her.

Maybe Malik didn't believe her because he had fabricated the shark story and her father's tales sounded mostly farfetched. "Yes. So one time, no wings, and the other yes, wings, but both times the boys told my father they were his guardian angels. So when my father was older—"

"Wait, how often did your dad get himself into trouble?" Malik asked.

"Often. So he was driving a car in the human world on an icy bridge. Stolen car. He had just gone for a joy ride as a teen. The car careened through the railing, and he hit his head so hard on the dash, he was knocked out. That time his guardian angel appeared in the car, woke him up, and told him to get out of there before the car crashed on the rocks below the cliffs and burst into flames."

"And he did."

"Yeah. I wouldn't be here if he hadn't."

Malik smiled. "Was that the last time?"

"Nope."

Malik laughed. "Okay, so your dad must be special to have had so many guardian angels rescue him over his lifetime."

"He was. Is. Anyway, I'm sure he's going to really be angry to learn I...uh, died." Which she really couldn't get a handle on. She looked perfectly normal, felt that way too. Then she gave Malik a scathing look. "Because my guardian angel wasn't there to save me. At least my father's guardian angels were always there for him."

"Yeah, I said I'm sorry. What else can I say? So what happened the last time?" Malik ran his hands through his hair and looked a bit remorseful.

"Aren't we ever going to reach Catriona's office?"

"Shortly."

They'd been walking through hall after hall, making a turn this way and that. She was so confused, she would never figure out a way back to her room from this maze of hallways.

"Well, my dad slipped through ice on a frozen lake. Everyone dared him he couldn't do it. My father always took dares to the extreme," she said.

"When was this? After the car incident?" Malik asked.

"Yeah, about a year later. Anyway, he fell through the ice, and he figured he would just fae transport back home, while creating all kinds of angst for the six teens who had been egging him on. They were all human, he thought, while he was the fae. What he hadn't counted on were the iron ore deposits in the soil under the water, and iron had leached into the water. He couldn't fae transport anywhere."

"So the trick was on him. I can't imagine any guardian angel could have saved him that time."

"Supposedly, the guardian angel transported a whole team of rescue workers to reach him. There were none in sight. And then—"

"He ended up in a human hospital when his guardian angel arrived."

"The guardian angel had actually been one of the teens standing on the shore with the others. He was saying, 'Don't do it, John. Don't do it.' He obviously hadn't tried very hard to stop my father from nearly losing his life."

"Aww, but here's the thing. We have to offer a teaching lesson and if the angel had only told your dad about the danger of the frozen lake, he might not have listened. But when your dad actually experienced the horror of nearly losing his life, then that's a different story. Did your dad ever pull that stunt again?"

"No. Once was enough."

"See?"

"Okay, I see your point. At least the angel had saved my father. At least my father's guardian angels were always there to rescue him. It's too bad mine wasn't."

Malik at least had the sense to look a little guilty again.

CHAPTER 3

"*H*ere is Catriona's office," Malik finally said, opening the door for her to an outer office where a receptionist motioned for Ariana to go inside.

When Ariana walked into Catriona's office, a woman with light brown skin and dark brown hair smiled at her. "I'm Catriona, and you are our most recent recruit into the Angel Corp. Have a seat and I'll explain your job to you."

Ariana knew to obey the commands of her king and queen, but this woman wasn't a hawk fae and she wasn't in charge of her. She folded her arms. "How can I earn whatever I need to so that I can return to the fae world as I knew it?"

Catriona frowned at her. "Who has been talking such nonsense to you? Malik?" Her words were spoken harshly, and Ariana worried Malik would get in trouble for it even though he had told her nothing. But just the way the woman spoke the words, Ariana knew there had to be some truth to the matter.

Ariana thought if she did something right—hopefully not wrong—she could return to her former way of life.

"Malik didn't tell me a thing about what I'm supposed to do or anything about being able to return to the fae world as a normal fae. Maybe there's not even a way to do it," Ariana said, though she suspected there was. Did Malik know about it? Why else would Catriona have suspected he told Ariana how to go about it if he didn't? Unless it was just because Malik had been sent to bring her here and Catriona thought he had been discussing it with Ariana and *that's* why Catriona had believed he had somehow learned of it and told Ariana.

"Have a seat," Catriona said. Gone was the sweetness Catriona had first exhibited when Ariana had arrived.

Ariana figured she had put herself on a "to be watched" list. She shouldn't have asked the head angel fae the question. Then again, if anyone knew the truth, it was probably someone who was in charge like her.

"You will have numerous missions to save fae or humans who are at risk of dying to prove you can handle the job. If you miss saving the victims too often, your situation will be reevaluated."

"And when I do, I can return to the fae world?" Ariana was determined to do this, and it wasn't a matter of if, but when.

The woman tilted her chin down like Ariana's mother had done when she was being a disruptive child. "No, but you'll be kicked out of the Angel Corp if you don't accomplish the mission. Believe me, you don't want that."

"So what's in it for me?" Ariana finally took a seat on the chair.

"You are an angel. A guardian angel. You should be proud of saving fae and humankind and not want for anything more."

At least in the hawk fae court, Ariana served in an honorable role. She'd saved King Tiernan several times from his enemies and Queen Ritasia twice. Ariana had been awarded medals, given special treatment, respected by all—except for the enemy fae who she had taken down. So she was used to doing good deeds for glory and for special compensation, and oh, sure, yeah, for doing what was right. She loved the royal family.

She didn't figure she would get any special treatment just because she did her job here.

This was the pits.

Ariana was sure she hadn't gotten off on the right foot with Catriona either. Note to self, don't ask the head angel questions that could get her into hot water. She sighed. "Okay, so what is it that you want me to do?"

"You saved a couple of kids from drowning. Let's see if you can do it again."

"Again?" After losing her own life in the Gulf, Ariana shuddered to think of going near open water again. Was that kind of like angel PTSD? Post Traumatic Stress Disorder? Had to be. She'd always loved the water before that. What if she got her wings wet and drowned again?

Since the woman wasn't forthcoming about how all this was supposed to go about, Ariana asked, "Okay, so what's the deal with the wings?" She pointed to her back. "I don't have any."

"They'll appear when you need them."

Great. If Ariana had wings, she wanted them to appear when she wanted them to. Like, to show off to other fae. To flutter them at a cute angel like the one who did that to her in the hall on the way here. Imagine some of her hawk fae friends seeing her now. No one would ever believe she would end up in the Angel Corp.

"Okay, so what if I need them when I'm supposed to be saving a drowning victim, and I get the wings wet? Wouldn't I just... drown? But worse, since I guess I can't really die again, I wouldn't save the victim?"

"They're waterproof, much like a duck's, but essentially, your job is to talk the potential victims out of getting themselves into trouble in the first place."

"So I'll look like an angel and tell them not to do whatever they're about to do."

"You will look like a human."

"And they won't listen to me. No one ever listens to me. And you know how people are"—just like she was—"if someone tells them they can't do it, they make a bigger effort to do it." This was going to be a lost cause, she could tell right now before she even tried to save anyone.

"Which is why you will have an extensive video training program. You're special, Ariana. You were meant for greatness. But you still have to earn the right to be here."

Special? No one had ever called her special. A special angel? Or a special something else?

"Watch the training videos showing our kind saving humans and fae. Study them. When you're ready, you'll go on your first assignment."

"I thought the victims would be in peril soon." Ariana was thinking like any second and she had no time to lose. Did it count if she didn't save them if Catriona didn't send her on her way in time?

"We have time. Malik will give you your first mission soon enough as soon as he feels you're ready. You'll get all the training you need from the videos. Though you have class assignments too."

"Class assignments?" Ariana hadn't had to go to school in ages and she worked hard to excel at things she loved to do, but this was something else. Forget that!

Catriona smiled, but the look wasn't sweet. "You want to do this right, don't you? You want to save the victims, correct? You want to stay with us a while longer, right? Then you need to prepare yourself for this new work. Just think of it like when you were learning to be a royal guard, the training, the rules concerning royal protocol. You weren't born knowing it, you know. You had to work at it."

True, but that was because Ariana had *wanted* to be a royal guard and wear their cool uniforms and be treated as almost royalty like her family had before her. Here? She was starting over and being a guardian angel wasn't something she had ever planned to do, even if she'd known angel fae had existed.

"All right. You have your work cut out for you. Run along." The director dismissed her with a flick of her wrist.

The receptionist came in and escorted Ariana out of the office because she hadn't moved fast enough for the director's taste. Then the receptionist gave Ariana four movie CDs and made her exit the outer office and into the hall, where Ariana's helpful Malik was leaning against the wall, arms folded across his chest, ready to walk her back to her room, she thought.

"You can see those in the viewing room. I'll watch them with you. We'll have popcorn and soda—" Malik said.

She raised her brows at him.

"Well, we can eat, sure, but we don't need to."

"Why would you need to see the movies again? Did you miss something? Forget something?" She didn't believe he would want to watch them for no other reason than he wanted to be with her when she viewed them. Or worse-case scenario, he had been given the task of ensuring she watched them in their entirety.

"I'm your angel mentor. If you have any questions about the movies, then I'll answer them for you, if I can."

"Why are you my angel mentor when you failed to save me as my angel guardian?"

"It's my punishment."

Well, she had asked an honest question and got an honest answer. "Thank you for being honest with me. So what are you supposed to do? Follow me all over the place and make sure I do whatever I'm supposed to be doing?" She could imagine that would be a real drag. Not that he was mentoring her, but more like a spy for the director.

"Yep. Because the director doesn't want you to fail. She says you're special."

"Special, how?"

"She wouldn't say. Don't you know?"

"I wouldn't be asking you if I knew, now would I?"

"True." Malik escorted her into the viewing room and a

redheaded guy in there quickly shut off the video he had been watching, his face turning crimson, and he smiled broadly at her.

She'd only gotten a glimpse of the video that had captured two angels with wings flapping slightly, kissing each other.

"Don't tell the director about that," the guy said, hurrying out of his seat. "Are you new?" He smiled brightly at Ariana.

"Booker, this is Ariana, and Ariana, stay away from him. He kisses all the angel fae."

"But I don't kiss and tell," Booker said.

Malik scoffed. "Yeah, but we catch you at it all the time, so we don't have to hear you tell about your exploits."

"Don't tell the director on me, okay?" Booker asked, sounding suddenly concerned.

"Since when have I ever told the director about your shenanigans?" Malik asked.

"Right, but I just wanted to be sure." Booker smiled again at Ariana and took her hand and kissed it. "'Til we meet again." Then he hurried out of there and Malik shut the door.

The room had chairs set up like human movie theaters she'd been to, with each row higher than the one before it in case several angels were here at one time, she suspected. The seats were pastel blue and looked comfy, the tables between them white polyurethane, and the walls of the amphitheater were covered in shimmery blue wallpaper. It made her think of being in some ethereal place that was modernistic in tone.

She sat on one of the middle seats at the top row.

"You sit up here so no one is behind you," Malik observed and sat beside her.

"I don't like people breathing down my neck. Though if I wanted to pull a fae trick in a human theater, I would sit where people could see me coming and going with my vanishing act, just for fun. But normally, I like to sit in back."

"And you like to know where all the exits are. You don't want to be hemmed in. You don't like enclosed spaces. You're claustrophobic."

Ariana stared at him, wondering how he knew so much about her when he didn't know her! "Just start the movie. And where's the popcorn? Buttered? Salted? I want the best."

A fae suddenly showed up with a bag of popcorn for both of them and her favorite carbonated cola. Malik was drinking a bottle of water.

"How did he know? Oh, don't tell me they listen to every word we're saying in here."

"No, I pressed a button over there on my chair handle and ordered two boxes of popcorn and your favorite drink."

She glanced down at the handle on her chair and saw that it had different drink options and several popcorn options, including no butter, no salt, and one that was caramel. Maybe she'd try the caramel one later.

She began eating the popcorn—which was just perfect—and watched the first movie.

A girl was wading in a tide pool, the water swiftly coming in. She wasn't paying attention to it and whoever was watching the girl wasn't paying attention to the little girl either. A woman was lying out on a chaise lounge nearby, tanning, nose in a book. The girl must have been about ten and the fae approached her saying, "The tide is coming in. Come, and we'll go see your parents."

The girl just stared at the angel as if she didn't know what to think of her. And then suddenly, the fae sprouted wings and the girl screamed and ran toward her parents, the currents filling the tidal pool within seconds, but the angel had vanished, and the girl was safe.

"Easy enough," Ariana said.

"They're not all that easy. You get to see the easy ones first and then they get to be more of a challenge. It gives you an idea of how to handle various scenarios, though all cases will be different. Humans, fae are all unique. They will react to someone trying to assist them differently. Take the girl. She could have loved angels and the sight of one would have made her hug her instead of running away in terror. The fae would have transported her to the family. She could have anyway. *We* also act differently in every situation. The angel fae was trying to take a less intrusive approach. Others might have just skipped trying to convince the child and moved her. But the key is that we're trying to impart a lesson. So just moving the child wouldn't have taught her the water, or tidal water, could be dangerous. She might not have learned anything from the experience. She might have needed to have been swept under and then rescued, for her to get the point. We don't know for sure how our help aids whoever we've saved in the long run."

"So you mean the kid could just go back to a tidal pool the next day and be at the same risk. Does the angel have to return and save her again?"

"No. Though it can happen again. But sometimes they're off saving someone else. Possibly the same thing was happening with your father."

"The concept that an angel is the guardian for an individual throughout their lives is bunk then."

"No. Sometimes a guardian angel is assigned to several different cases. Sometimes one is either assigned to an individual for their lifetime, while accomplishing other missions along the way, and other times, an angel has a particular fondness for the individual and selects him or her to continue to protect, mostly because the person is in danger throughout their life."

"Not through their own misdeeds though."

"Not necessarily. Parents that don't take care of them when they're young, fighting in a war, when they're older, working on jobs that are dangerous later. It doesn't mean the person is a daredevil and puts himself at risk, but that the kind of life he lives is just geared that way."

"Wow, okay." Ariana started the next movie, realizing these

weren't long movies showing someone's whole lifetime, but cameo appearances of angels saving someone's life.

She watched as two teens were getting ready to bungee jump off a bridge, signs all over stating it was illegal to do it, which made it all the more worthwhile to risk their necks over it.

The angel—had to be because he suddenly appeared—and she wondered then if all angel stories were recorded for features that would train future angels. He was standing off to the side, not wearing a harness to bungee jump and he jumped up on the railing, no wings on display and said, "No need to use a harness. Just jump."

The guys laughed at him.

"Yeah, you first," the one teen said.

And that made Ariana angry. "Why even save the kid if he's going to be that rotten? What if he told some kid to jump off a bridge like that who wasn't an angel and then the kid did it and died? By the way, who is filming these cases?"

"A documentary angel fae."

The angel dove off the bridge. The teens' mouths were agape, and they both hurried to look over the railing, but the angel was gone.

Ariana's mouth gaped.

"Holy crap, you saw what I saw, didn't you?" the one redheaded kid said.

"Yeah, the guy just jumped. And he's…he's not there."

"Did he get up and walk away?" the redhead said.

Suddenly, the angel appeared on the bridge again. "It's not safe to bungee jump off the bridge."

The teens swung around to see the angel walking toward them. Their eyes were as round as soccer balls. They weren't saying a word now.

Ariana ate some more of her popcorn. This was just getting good. More like fae behavior. She smiled.

"There's a reason the bridge is off-limits for bungee jumping. Two kids died here doing that," the angel fae said.

"They...they didn't know what they were doing."

"Your rope is too long. You'll hit the ground before you know it. You know how hard those rocks are? Bash your legs and spine and skull against them and you'll know." The angel kept walking toward them, and they were backing up, looking like they were going to run, like they were seeing a ghost. But he kept walking.

"Hey, back off, guy," one of the teens said, trying to show his bravado, but it was slipping fast.

The angel ignored them and walked straight through them and continued walking until he faded away.

Ariana chuckled. "I like his style."

The teens watched in the direction the angel had gone, not moving a muscle.

"So are they going to give it up or not?" she asked.

Malik smiled, continued to eat his popcorn, and wouldn't tell her the end of the story.

She figured it had to have a happily ever after or they wouldn't be using it as a training film.

The redhead said to his friend, "Let's go to that other bridge."

"The one I told you about earlier today. I told you I wanted to go there."

"Yeah, well, it's legal and...I don't know about you, but this one is just creepy."

Then the two hurried to pack their gear into their dusty, black pickup, jumped in, and tore off down the road.

The angel returned, gave a bow, and smiled for the camera, then vanished and that was the end of the story.

"I think that was Leesa recording it," Malik says.

"A girlfriend? So angels can date?

"Not exactly."

"Well then what exactly?" Ariana asked, tired of this cryptic business with Malik.

"Angel fae are here to save victims, not to start up where they left off in the fae world. Dating isn't really part of our mission, and the mission always comes first."

"Okay, so that means I can't date you."

Malik let out his breath.

She changed the subject. "These are all feel-good stories then that I have to watch. Do they ever show where mistakes were made?"

"Those are coming up. It's to show how things can go wrong and how we need to correct how we respond in a situation and take a different approach." Malik shrugged. "We win some, we lose some."

An eerie chill slid down her body. "You mean like with you failing to save me."

"Yeah, like with you."

She frowned at him. "I'm not in one of these films, am I?"

"Yeah. Well, I am. It's my story, not yours. It shows the mistake I made and how I need to rectify the situation in the future if I am to save the one I'm supposed to save."

"But that means losing someone else."

"Who wasn't scheduled to be saved."

"That's just not right."

"We have a limited number of angels available. We can't save every Tom, Dick, or Harry. It's just not feasible."

Then the movie started, featuring *It's a Wonderful Life.*

"Wait, this is a human movie!"

"Right, but it's supposed to be a little bit of a diversion for those who have to watch all these angel fae rescues."

She finished her popcorn. "Okay, so are we supposed to glean anything from this movie?"

"Sure, that if we don't save the person, how it can affect a whole bunch of people, and if they had never been born, how that would affect a ton of outcomes."

"Uhm, like me—you not saving me in time."

"Yeah. Like that. Now you're a guardian angel and instead of just protecting the hawk fae royal family, you can protect a multitude of other people."

That made her wonder if she could return to see who had taken her place at the royal court.

"So is there a way to return to our former lives?" she asked, casually like.

He sighed and shook his head. "Just concentrate on doing what you're told to do, and you won't be banished."

"You're evasive every time I ask you the question. That means you know how to do it, or you know some who have done so. Don't you want to return to your former existence? Wait, what do you mean by I can be banished?"

CHAPTER 4

*M*alik knew Ariana was going to be an issue. He still wondered why she was considered special. And no, he didn't want to return to his former existence when all he'd ever wanted was to be with her. Then he frowned. Had he made the mistake of trying to save the human male because he'd really wanted Ariana not to make it so she could be an angel like himself, and they could be together in this way?

He didn't want to think too deeply into the matter.

"I think you do know how to return to our former lives but you're afraid that someone you don't trust—which could be anyone —would tell on you if you revealed the truth. Your secret is safe with me. And really, if you know of a way to return to our world, I'll do it with you. Unless it's better to do it on a solo basis," Ariana said.

And then what? As soon as she was back with the hawk fae, would she have anything to do with him? No.

He thought he would give up on wanting to get to know her better, but he was hopelessly hooked on her.

She turned to look at him and he quickly averted his gaze. "You're supposed to be watching the movie."

"So the angel wants to earn his wings. We already have them, right? Or at least some of us do."

"Right. Watch the movie." He leaned back in his chair. He would hate taking her to the movies. He could imagine her talking during the whole movie just as much as she was now.

The movie finally ended, and she was done for the day, so she said.

"You have to watch the rest of the first training missions."

"This is angel rescue overload."

"You know most new angels are eager to take on their first assignments. They can't wait to finish all the training so they can go do a mission."

"I guess I'm not like your typical guardian angel then." She leaned her recliner back and started to watch the next video.

A woman had a baby in a stroller, a preschooler pushing it, and the woman had paused to text someone on her phone. The young girl was pushing the stroller toward a busy intersection and not stopping.

Ariana tensed and Malik knew she wanted to rescue the two children. She had the nurturing, protective instincts, but she just didn't want to do the whole angel thing, he suspected.

This was his favorite rescue. There was no sense in talking to the mother. It would have taken too long. He did knock the phone out of her hand, and he wanted her to see the disaster waiting to happen. Instead of seeing her kids in danger, she'd been upset about her phone flying out of her hand, landing on the concrete, and the glass cracking. It served her right for not watching out for her kids.

"That's you!" Ariana said.

"Yeah, one of my finer moments."

Then he transported to where the kids were and put on the stroller brakes. The young child couldn't move the stroller and the woman finally looked to see the little girl struggling to move it, but she wasn't having any success. The woman finally ran to them and that was the end of the story.

"You were invisible to the humans the whole time."

"Right. You don't have to show yourself to get a point across or to save a human, or a fae."

"Okay, so good job."

"Thanks."

"You broke the woman's phone."

"Yep." He felt that was one of the best moments during the mission. Of course stopping the kids from crossing the dangerous road was too. But the other was a perfectly acceptable fae move.

"Instead of rescuing the kids first."

"I had time. I would have been there for them in a heartbeat and just blocked them from crossing the street, but if we can do more subtle methods and use our intelligence to solve the problem—like locking the stroller's wheels—even better."

"Very clever."

"Thank you."

"You didn't mug it up for the camera."

"This is serious business," he said.

The next movie was of a fae snowboarding in an area that had signs posted all over warning it was avalanche territory.

"Okay, so should we be saving people who don't have enough sense and disobey rules, like the bungee bridge jumpers—"

Malik shook his head. "He's a fae. We ignore human rules and conventions."

"True. But if he's going to be so stupid to pull that, why should anyone be sent to rescue him?"

"Ours is not to reason why—"

"Ours is to do and die?" Ariana sounded miffed.

He smiled. "It's just the first part of the sentence that's important. We don't question why we have to do what we have to do. We just do it and hope that someone at the top is making the right decisions. Maybe the fae on the snowboarder does something for our people in the future that saves tons of fae? What do I know? Exactly why did you save those kids in the Gulf anyway? You're a fae. You shouldn't have felt anything for them. For one of our own kind, sure," Malik said.

"Oh, yeah, and that's why you tried to save the man, right?"

Malik rubbed his chin thoughtfully. "I didn't want to interrupt what you were doing. You looked like you had the other kid in hand. You would have felt defeated if I had interfered and given you a hand instead. If I had known... Well, I hadn't or I would have done my job," he told her. He'd had other options, but he'd opted to babysit her. He couldn't explain his fascination for her.

Maybe because she'd been chosen as one of the hawk fae king's elite royal guard like he'd been one for the phantom fae kingdom. Maybe because she had tried to save the kids and had done so at great peril to herself and drowned. Maybe because when she went to the beach with her girlfriend, she was always alone while her girlfriend easily picked up boyfriends and left Ariana on her own. Yet Ariana continued to accompany her and spent the time looking out to sea or watching others having fun —swimming, sailing, parasailing, building sandcastles.

While *he* had watched *her*. He sighed. "Do you want to have a break? I couldn't watch all these in one sitting if I'd tried. We can meet another couple of angels."

"Yeah, like I'd said before. By the way, what happened when I drowned? Did the humans fish me out of the water? Did the fae recover my body and return me home to have a funeral? Was Claude there to throw flowers on my grave? Even though we'd broken up before I drowned, it would have been a nice gesture."

"You were lost at sea. Sorry."

"What?" Ariana sounded furious.

"Uh, yeah, I really am sorry. I tried to find your body, but you just weren't there. And then when I returned to Angel Central, I learned you were here. Of course Catriona was upset with me because I hadn't found your body and recovered it for your own people to take care of."

"Sooo, they could think I'm still alive."

"All reports stated that you drowned, and your body was never found."

"Human reports, right? I could have just transported home."

"You didn't." He frowned at her, knowing where she was going with this line of reasoning.

"If no one reported that I had drowned—I mean, the fae, like my friend Charity hadn't seen me drown because I could have gotten tired of waiting for her to finish flirting with the human boys, I could have just been sidetracked from going home."

"In the job you hold? You would never have been that sidetracked. You know how important it was to you."

Ariana felt she was in an emotional whirlwind of turmoil. How could no one know what had happened to her? That she was truly dead? Her father would be devastated. Though she still thought it could suit her purposes because she could do what she needed to do and earn her way back to the fae world, she was sure of it.

And take up her old job. But then she'd have to make up some wild story about how she had been abducted by angels, or aliens, or something, which was the reason she never showed back up for work. She groaned. They would probably have replaced her with someone else by now. Paul, she bet. He'd been vying for her job even before she got it, telling her she only got it because she was friends with the hawk fae queen and that she had only been friends with her to get the position!

Yeah, Paul would for sure have her job by now. And if she showed up late for it, the hawk fae king would not let her have her job back. Unless Paul failed to save the king. No, that wouldn't work because then someone else would be king, should the queen remarry, and he would choose his own royal guard.

What did Charity think about Ariana going missing? Did she

believe she might wash up on some beach at some time or another? Or turn up on some yacht, having the greatest time of her life? Or that she was having a fling with a guy and forgot all about the time?

Ariana glanced at Malik. He smiled at her. She sighed. "Okay, so when I go back to the fae world, I guess I'll have to get a new job."

"You're an angel."

"I know, but when I earn my fae status back and when I return to the fae world, I will have to make some adjustments in my life."

"They didn't have a funeral for you because they still feel you'll come back," Malik said, sounding reluctant to mention it.

"Okay, so it won't be a shock when I show up."

"Yeah, it will, because you're never late to your job and you've been gone for three days."

"Three days? No way. Three whole days?"

"Yep. I...we didn't think you would ever wake up. Catriona said you would, but the rest of us weren't sure."

"Did it take you that long to wake up here?"

"Four days, so you beat me by a day."

She smiled.

"Are you always that competitive?" he asked, as they left the theater and he walked her outside in the fresh air and sunshine, the clouds floating high above in the blue sky.

"I will make it back to the fae world before you do."

Malik laughed and walked her over to a rooftop garden over-looking mist-covered mountains and waterfalls rushing into rivers way down below. Then he motioned to a couple of angels standing nearby about their age. "That is Elwin and you already met Juno," Malik said to Ariana, introducing her to the others. "Meet Ariana, one of our newest members of the Corp."

Elwin snorted. "How did you end up getting a newbie to

TERRY SPEAR

babysit?" He had curly black hair and blue eyes that took in her whole appearance and then he shook his head.

"I didn't save her when I was supposed to."

Juno said, "Hey, nice to see you again."

"Do you have a support group here for fae who have expired way before their time?" Ariana asked.

Elwin laughed, like he thought it was the dumbest thing he'd ever heard.

"For new angels, not for the likes of you," Ariana said, irritated with the fae. She was brand new at this. What did she know? And she would have to ask, unless someone would tell her upfront. She supposed she should have just asked Malik in private sometime, but he was smiling at her too. "What? You don't think we might have some issues with being here?"

"Come on. I'll give you your first assignment," Malik said to Ariana. "A really simple one. Catriona might have told you that you'd have schoolwork to do."

"Good luck," Juno said.

"Don't screw it up and give us a bad name," Elwin said.

Then Malik transported Ariana to a private home with a swimming pool and deposited her in the backyard. Large palm trees lined the back of the property and big windows looked out on the pool.

Finally, Ariana was given a simple case to work on. But she was surprised Malik had given her the assignment. "I thought Catriona would give me all my missions."

"No. She does it for the really special angels who have worked here for a long time. A newbie like you? You've got me. You have five cases to accomplish satisfactorily to prove you're up to the task. They go from the very simplest in the beginning and graduate to the most difficult. But not like the ones the special angels have to take care of."

"And then if I can accomplish all of my tasks, I can return to the fae world?"

"You don't get it, do you? You're here. Stuck with us. You have a new job. You're no longer a royal guard. Get used to it. If you screw up, you leave, but it won't be the way you want to go. This is your home unless you prove you can't handle it."

"I can handle it. Them." But she still wanted an acceptable reward! And to her, that meant returning to her world.

Ariana didn't know what to think as she watched the young girl playing by the pool. She knew, if she was supposed to be her guardian angel, the little girl was going to fall into the pool, right? Yep, there she went. Bouncing a ball around poolside, no adults in sight, no one to stop her. Nothing to keep her from going into the pool.

Ariana looked around to see who was watching the young girl. A woman in the kitchen was gabbing on the phone, washing dishes, glancing out the window, but not really seeing what Ariana was seeing.

So what was Ariana supposed to do? Sprout wings and carry the girl back inside the house? She wanted to and she wanted to tell the woman how she could lose her daughter—if she was her daughter—in the blink of an eye.

Ariana wasn't visible to the young girl, maybe about three or four years old or so. She knew, from all the videos she'd watched, she was supposed to give the guardian of the child a real scare so that the parent wouldn't do anything like this again. But Ariana couldn't help fearing the worst. That she might accidentally miss getting the child out of danger in time and lose her. Then what?

She would have failed her first mission, but who cared about a stupid mission anyway? The child's life was at stake. Which made her think about Malik not saving her life when he was supposed to, and that irritated her.

Ariana hovered close to the girl, not taking any chances. She sure hoped this time her wings would appear and help her out. She envisioned swooping down and pulling the girl out of the water and setting her back on the pool patio where she would cry her eyes out and then the guardian would come out to see what the matter was.

"You can't wear your wings in the water," Malik said.

The girl glanced around to see who was talking to her.

Ariana gaped at him. "You weren't supposed to be here. I thought. This is my job, and you weren't supposed to help."

"I'm not helping. I'm just observing."

"Catriona said the wings are like duck wings."

The girl was looking all about, trying to find where the voices were coming from.

At least she was distracted from going too near the water. Then again, if Ariana didn't save her, the mother would be unaware that her daughter had been in danger. The child would still not perceive a threat and would likely do this again some other time when Ariana wasn't here.

"You're messing up everything for me," Ariana said, telepathically this time. *"Why are you here?"*

"I have to see how you would do with your assignments."

"Famously."

When they stopped speaking so the girl could hear them, the breeze rolled the ball into the water. At least Ariana had kept her eyes on the preschooler and not on the angel fae who was annoying her.

The girl did just what Ariana was afraid she'd do. She ran toward the water to get her ball. Ariana moved to intercept her. After the last situation where she tried to save a girl and had successfully done so but drowned herself in the process, she realized she couldn't do it! She couldn't get into the water. She couldn't do it.

"Malik, if she gets into the water, I can't save her."

"You have to. It's your job, your mission. I can't interfere."

Ariana saw the girl run straight off the edge of the pool and into the water, paddled hopelessly for a second or two and went under.

"Do something, Malik!" Ariana screamed at him.

But he didn't budge. "You will have to face your fears. I had to."

Ariana gritted her teeth and jumped into the water, and realized it was only a couple of feet deep, which shocked and irritated her at the same time. Though she had to admit she'd felt a hint of relief too. She pulled the child out of the water and set her on the side of the pool. The little girl was coughing and hacking. Ariana was certain if the scenario had been different, at the beach, for instance, she would have panicked even worse. The woman in the house was running outside to reach the child.

"You should have never been near the pool!" the woman screamed and grabbed the girl up and hugged her, tears running down the woman's cheeks as she rushed her inside, the girl crying now.

Right, the girl should never have been near the pool when she didn't have an adult watching her.

"Some help you were," Ariana said to Malik. She was dripping wet and was glad it was a warm day.

"Yeah, well this business is a case of sink or swim. I told you it was the simplest case you could take care of for the first time." They heard the garage door open and then the car backed out and took off down the road. "She's probably taking her to the hospital to get her seen to."

"At least she's doing that," Ariana said, annoyed.

"I believe you've probably sufficiently solved the case—saved the child, taught the mother a lesson, and all is well."

Ariana scoffed. "No thanks to you." She was so irritated with Malik. Then he transported her to the door of her room. She stepped inside and closed the door, not saying goodbye. She realized the room had its own bathroom. She was glad for that. She could imagine having to go down these long halls to find a bathroom to take a shower and such. She grabbed a towel and dried her hair. Then she pulled off her wet clothes and looked through the wardrobe. All white lacy wear, as if she was supposed to portray the image of an angel. And she still hadn't once seen any sign of her angel wings. But she'd noticed she was the only one who had to wear all white. A newbie thing?

Were there even any other new angel fae here? Shouldn't she at least meet them?

CHAPTER 5

*I*n the middle of drying off and dressing, someone knocked on Ariana's door. She hurried to pull on her shirt. "Hold on!"

When she reached the door, she was surprised to see Juno. "Hey, how was your first assignment?" Juno asked.

Terrifying. Because Ariana had been afraid of the water when she hadn't ever been before.

Before Ariana could respond, Juno said, "Malik says you were afraid of the water when you had to save a little girl who fell into a pool."

Then why ask Ariana how she had done!

"You know he couldn't help you. Do you want to go swimming?"

Ariana frowned at her.

Juno walked her outside. "We have a pool. They have it for angels who need to save victims in the water. It's great for practicing rescues and for overcoming fear of the water. Just so you know, Malik did the same thing with his first case, nearly didn't save the victim because he had drowned like you had and was afraid it would happen again. We have to face our fears. Take me. I hate flying. I'm terrified of heights. The first time I had to save a victim falling from a cliff, I was catatonic. Do you know why?"

"Was that how you died?"

"Yep. I was locked in a tower for—misbehaving and I couldn't transport in the fae way. Iron bracelets had been welded around my ankles. It didn't faze me. I would just climb down the wall of the tower. There were lots of finger and toe holds, I assumed. Vines too. I figured easy-peasy. Was I ever mistaken. The next thing I know, I'm here, lucky to be here really, and not buried in the ground somewhere. So yeah, before that, I had no trouble with heights. Afterward, all I remembered was falling, falling, falling, splat."

"Oh, how awful." Ariana thought that would be a worse way to go. "So, yeah, you could teach me to overcome my fear of water. Though I might not be as afraid of pools as I am of the Gulf or the ocean."

Juno arched her brows.

"Well, for the first time since I drowned, yeah, I was afraid of the water. I didn't realize I would be either. I think that was the worst of it. And I can help you overcome your fear of heights, if you would like."

Juno showed her wings off. "I have wings now and once I learned how to use them, I felt more secure about heights. Watch for downdrafts, no using while in the water, we're not ducks or some other kind of waterbird, and be careful of being seen with them. You don't know how often I've wanted to show them off to humans. Or fae even. They're pretty cool."

"Catriona said they were waterproof," Ariana said.

Juno ran her hand over one of her wings. "Well, maybe the longer you have them they are. I guess I always just thought they were like other birds' wings that aren't waterbirds."

Elwin joined them on the patio. "Are you telling her that old story of yours about your fear of heights and flying? Don't believe it. When she fell from the tower, she didn't remember anything about it."

"Says you," Juno said.

"So how did *you* die?" Ariana asked Elwin, since he was such a smart aleck about everything.

"I got too close to a lion."

"A lion? Don't tell me you went into the lion's den at the zoo or met up with one in Africa and thought to show how cool you were." At least Ariana had tried to save someone when she had drowned.

"Of course not." Elwin's tone was haughty. "How do you think we end up here anyway? We try to save a life."

Oh, she hadn't expected him to say that. "So what happened? Did you save the life?"

"Yeah. Don't you know how all this works? You've got to save a life before you perish, or you don't end up here. I shouldn't have gotten involved, really. I was along for the ride on a Safari photo shoot, just chilling, watching the photographers get up close and personal with the lion and lionesses in the one pride. They were shooting with telephoto zoom lenses, but even so, when the lion came to investigate, the one photographer didn't want the lion to eat his camera. He was foolish enough to try and chase it away."

"And you were foolish enough to try and save him," Juno said.

"I had a moment of stupidity, I will admit."

"One?" Juno rolled her eyes.

"Wait, if each of us tried to save someone before we met our end, then how did you end up here?" Ariana asked Juno. "Since you hadn't saved anyone. You just fell off a tower."

"She didn't tell you the best part?" Elwin tsked.

"Okay, so another fae was locked in the tower in another room, and hers was above mine. She was climbing down, and I heard her. I went to investigate, peered out the window, and realized she was making her escape. She gave me the idea to climb down too. But when I came out of the window and started to grab hold of a vine, she fell and nearly knocked me off the wall. I grabbed her with one hand and shoved her into the open window of my room and fell. I hadn't planned to fall, you know. I knew I would make it down just fine. If she hadn't given me the idea to climb, I wouldn't have put myself in harm's way."

"And you wouldn't have saved her," Ariana said.

"True."

"So why were you incarcerated in the tower in the first place?" Ariana asked.

"You sure ask a lot of questions," Juno said.

"As one of the royal guards for the hawk fae king, I was used to asking a lot of questions."

Juno laughed. "You're just like us. Only you're an Angel Newbie Class, nothing special. No lofty position. You're not working for royalty—for a king."

"So why were you incarcerated?" Ariana knew how to handle evasive people in her line of work.

"I stole from a fae. It was a…property dispute."

"Sounds to me like they didn't take your side in the case."

Juno smiled. "The dispute I had was with a royal princess. You know how that goes. Whoever has the crown is the one who is believed."

"Oh, okay, yeah, sorry." Not that Ariana totally believed Juno, but then again, she could see her point. Though she thought the hawk fae king might figure something was going on with his daughter, if he had one, if that ever had come up in their kingdom.

"Do you want to go swimming?" Juno asked again.

"Yeah sure. Do we have swimming suits?"

"Yeah, anything you need is in your room. I'll meet you at the pool then. It's right over there." Juno motioned off toward two pillars and an archway. Are you coming?" Juno asked Elwin.

"I know how to swim and I'm not afraid of the water. But if

you want to go tower climbing, I'll go with you." Elwin smiled at her.

"I have wings now. I don't have a fear of flying or tower climbing now. I can just use my wings."

"I haven't seen mine yet." Ariana couldn't help that she was a little disappointed. Then she left to dress in a swimsuit.

After that she made her way to the pool, but she saw only Elwin standing poolside, wearing blue board shorts featuring a great white shark with all its vicious, sharp teeth on display.

"Where is everybody?" Ariana asked.

"They're coming. You know you'll never get over your fear of the Gulf or the ocean by swimming in a pool. You have to really immerse yourself in the proper environment to get the feel of it if you're going to ever save anyone in it."

"Like you know all about it. What? Are you the head angel shrink?"

Elwin smiled wickedly. She should have known that some fae were better left alone and shouldn't be taunted.

Well, she wasn't going to wait around for Juno to show up all day. Ariana studied the crystal blue water, the breeze making little ripples of waves on the surface. She could do this. Even without the incentive of saving anyone drowning in the water. She could dive in, and she would be fine. Hating to admit it, Elwin was probably right. If she had to jump into a stormy sea, she'd be hesitant, reluctant, and scared to pieces. But she could do this. She glanced around and looked for Juno, but she wasn't in sight.

"Now or never," Elwin said.

She wanted to slap him. Swimming had been like second nature to her. She couldn't imagine living in a desert. She loved all things water. Maybe because the hawk fae kingdom had so many lakes, and the ocean wasn't far away.

She could do this. Then she was going to do her most perfect dive form and anticipated feeling the silky warm water caressing her skin, being swallowed up and luxuriating in it like she normally would have done—pre-drowning in the water. But Elwin shoved her into the pool instead and she was submersed instantly, then swam to the surface.

She could have socked him! After she got over her annoyance with him, the water was just as she had expected as she came up for air. Warm, silky, crystal clear, looking blue and then it was dark, briny water, salty and fishy smelly and much colder, a shock to her system. She instantly witnessed her worst nightmare unfolding.

She was no longer in the pool in the surrealistic world of the guardian angel fae, but in the frothing ocean as a massive storm headed her way. And she couldn't transport herself out of there no matter how hard she tried! She would kill Elwin!

The waves were growing in volume, and she saw no one out here but herself. Off in the distance, massive black clouds were moving toward her as if straight line winds were pushing them in a race to reach her.

"Elwin!" She was in the water! She proved she could do it, hadn't she? That she hadn't died of a heart attack as soon as she realized she wasn't in Kansas anymore?

Sheets of white light illuminated the black clouds, forks of lightning spearing the dark water below it, the crackling of thunder an ominous warning. Anyone dumb enough to be out here was risking his life.

And then she saw her worst nightmare. Okay, so her second worst nightmare, because being in the water with an approaching storm and the waves already swelling with the increased winds was definitely her first nightmare. But as she rose on a swell, she saw a capsized canoe in the distance.

Were there survivors? If she didn't save someone, she would really kill Elwin when she got back. If she got back. Ohmigod, what if she had gotten her wish and she wasn't a guardian fae any longer and she died again? That would be the pits. Especially if they didn't return her to the Angel Corp. So much for being special.

But she was already making the long—seemingly impossible —swim toward the overturned, yellow canoe. "Hey!" She meant to make contact with the paddle or paddlers because if she was swimming her heart out only to find the canoe was empty and the people in it had already drowned, then why hurry? But she did have the notion she could at least overturn the canoe—hopefully—and climb into it without capsizing it again, and make it to the shore. Then she could go somewhere for a nice, hot latte. She could see the shore off in the distance. The hotels. The people on the beach racing for the hotels, dragging umbrellas, kids, beach towels, and sand pails, the wind whipping the sand all across the beach, sand blasting everyone in its path.

Then she was in the trough of the waves again and couldn't see anything but water and more water. A rogue wave grew higher and higher behind her, and she was really hoping she *couldn't* drown again.

She swallowed a mouthful of water, and coughed and hacked, right before the wave slammed down on top of her and she disappeared into the briny deep, struggling in the churning water to rise to the surface again. She finally broke free, took a breath of air and saw she was a little closer to the canoe—the wind and waves propelling her toward it. But the black clouds were growing closer, the lightning strikes nearer by and the resounding thunder booming sooner and stronger every time the sheets of lightning lit up the sky. Or the forks of electrical charges dove into the water.

She had to reach the paddler, if he or she was still alive, before the lightning struck them. Not to mention the water was colder and the paddler could be suffering from hypothermia if he was in the water still and alive. Of course.

She continued to swim, continued to be pounded by white-capped waves, coming up for air, coughing up the sea, and trying again. She was persistent when she had to meet a self-imposed goal if nothing else. She knew she was on her own.

She was about there, the rain from the storm slamming into her in sheets, making everything appear gray—the sky, the water, the shore, the hotels, the canoe even that she would glimpse when she was riding the crest of a wave. Then she would fall into the bottom of the deep trough again and she felt she was lost in a world of water for all eternity.

But when she crested the next wave, she saw a dorsal fin swimming parallel to the canoe and that nearly had her heart stopping. Could things get any worse? Well, yeah, she was sure of it if she ran into a dead body, or someone who was alive being eaten by a shark!

Wasn't she supposed to be on a very simple mission for her second time out? She hoped Elwin would be stripped of his wings and thrown into the darkest dungeon.

She had been working hard to get to the canoe, but now that there was a shark circling it, she wasn't sure what to do. Head to shore, swimming way around the canoe? Anything to stay out of the shark's path. But what if someone was still clinging to life? Maybe underneath the canoe, holding on to one of the seats?

She couldn't be eaten by a shark, she told herself as she swam toward the canoe. *She couldn't be eaten by a shark.* She was a guardian angel. She couldn't die again. *She couldn't be eaten by a shark.* At least that's what she kept telling herself.

She couldn't identify what kind it was, not that it really mattered. They could all be eating machines. And then it was gone. Swimming around beneath the canoe? On the other side of the canoe? Looking for survivors like she was?

She was getting closer to the canoe now, watching for signs of the shark, and she finally managed to call out, "Hey! Is anyone there?"

If not, she was skipping the canoe and swimming for shore.

"Hey!" a man said, his voice weak.

Ohmigod, there was someone on the other side of the canoe.

"Hold on! I'm coming to get you!" And how would that work out? Really? How was she supposed to save a drowning man when she couldn't do anything—like fae transport, for heaven's sake!

Then two dorsal fins appeared, side by side, one shark a little ahead of the other. Great. See? That's what she figured. Things could get worse and—a rogue wave crashed over her at that point, and she went under.

Okay, yeah, they got even worse.

She clawed at the water to resurface, coughing and gasping for air. Then she finally reached the boat between shark circles, or at least they were somewhere that she couldn't see their dorsal fins. Then she felt something bump into her in the water. A dolphin. A playful dolphin. No way was she going to imagine it was one of the sharks, but she was sure it was.

"Nearly there!" she choked out, her mouth tasting of briny water.

She finally grabbed hold of the boat. "I'm here. I'm coming around to your side."

She was exhausted. She didn't realize that angels would get this much of a workout. She had always thought—if they truly existed—that they would have been all powerful, not feeling fae like distress or muscle aches, or all the fear she was feeling right now. Would it fade with time as she accomplished more and more of these missions?

If she'd been a fae, well, non-angel type, she would have been out of here already using her fae transport. "What's your name?" She thought she should get the paddler talking so he didn't give up hope.

"Michael. Who are you?" he asked.

"I'm your guardian angel."

He let out a muffled chuckle.

Yeah, some guardian angel, right?

She finally rounded the bow of the canoe and saw a drop-dead gorgeous guy wearing a long-sleeved wetsuit, at least, so he wouldn't be as cold as if he'd been wearing just swim trunks.

She continued to work her way around to him, holding onto the canoe the best she could.

"How are you going to save me?" His eyes were just as dark as Malik's but he had short blond hair.

If she'd just been the fae and not a guardian angel, she would have asked him out on a date! She didn't think an angel could do that.

"I don't know. Can we overturn the canoe together?" she asked.

"Yeah. I've tried, but every time I do, the waves get the best of me. Maybe together we can. We need to get underneath the canoe first. Then we'll continue to tread water and together, raise the one side of the canoe above the water to break the suction. Then we have to shove the canoe up hard and fast on the raised side of the canoe to flip it over and hope the waves don't prevent us from doing so."

"Okay, I'm game." She would try anything to get them out of the shark-infested waters.

"All right."

They both grabbed the gunwales of the canoe and Michael said, "One, two, three, go!"

Together they lifted the canoe and broke the suction. It was harder than she thought it would be, probably because a wave rammed the canoe just as they went to push it up and flip it over. They lost hold of the canoe and had to try again.

"One, two, three, go!" he said.

She was exhausted. He was exhausted. They managed to break the suction and then paused, holding it, hoping they could push it over when another wave rolled under them and lifted them high.

"Go!" Michael yelled.

Forget about the one, two, three. It was time, and they managed to flip the boat over into a trough. "Yes!" she shouted.

But another wave was coming, the rain still pouring down on top of them, and the lightning still lighting up the sky in a frightening way.

"Okay, swim quickly to the bow and then get on the other side. You'll climb in at the same time I do, but I'll be on this side at the stern. We have to do it simultaneously to keep the weight balanced or we'll flip it again," he warned.

"Okay." Or the waves would. She was glad her father had taught her all about the parts of a boat since he loved to boat and fish.

She made her way to the bow, spying the one shark's dorsal fin again. She wondered if Michael had seen them. She sure wasn't going to tell him about them if he hadn't.

"Hurry," Michael said.

She was hurrying! She'd expended so much energy swimming to him and his canoe, she didn't think she had much left.

Then she finally reached the bow, trying to catch her breath, and moved to the opposite side. "A giant of a rogue wave is coming, Michael, hurry!"

"Get ready to climb aboard. Go!"

She was struggling to get into the boat, and finally collapsed into the center where he was already lying on his side. She was on her belly, the rainwater pelting them.

"No paddle," he said with regret. "I lost both of them when I flipped over."

"Did you know about the storm?"

"Yeah, but it wasn't coming in until later. I was heading in when the waves got to be too much, and a rogue—"

The boat was beginning to lift on one side, and they rode the top of the swell and down into a trough. She didn't want to look and see if any really bad waves were going to crash into them.

"The rogue wave hit the canoe and capsized me. I couldn't

right it, not with all the waves pounding me. Not until I had your help. You truly are a guardian angel." He wiped a wet curl out of her eyes. "Did you see the sharks?" he asked.

Okay, so since he brought it up—"Yeah, I didn't want to mention it in case you panicked at the news. Things were bad enough already."

"They still are."

How well she knew. They could still be capsized, sink—the way the rainwater and waves were filling the boat—or get struck by lightning.

"I think I hear a motor." She sat up in the middle of the boat, stretching out to hold unto the gunwales on each side to keep her balance in the rocking canoe.

Michael sat up and smiled. "Hallelujah! A rescue mission at hand. Hey"—he looked back at her and frowned—"if you don't have anything better to do, can I buy you a lunch? You did save my life after all."

She would feel more like she had saved him once he was inside a building safe from the threat of the lightning storm.

"Yeah, I would love that." She was sure that wasn't a guardian angel thing to do, but she was all for it, if she could get away with it.

Then he leaned down to kiss her, and she thought how romantic! She leaned forward and he pressed his cold, blue lips against her own very cold mouth and hoped they could warm each other and put some color back into their lips. This was the nicest, most welcome kiss she had ever had and then she saw the rubber rescue raft getting closer, the men ready to take them in. She was so looking forward to having lunch with Michael, though he'd have to get her some clothes, and she'd have to shower at his place, because she couldn't just use her fae abilities to pop in here or there.

She was going to tell him she wasn't staying here, that she needed something to wear, that—

And suddenly she wasn't there in the canoe with him, drenched by rain, lightning all around them, cold winds whipping over them, getting rescued. She was sitting on a chaise lounge by the pool, covered in the briny sea mixed with rainwater, looking like a drowned rat, she figured.

"Ohmigod," Juno said, while Ariana was still trying to get her bearings. "What happened to you? We wasted hours looking for you. I didn't think you could fae transport. Where in the world did you go?"

Elwin was standing nearby, smiling.

"Ask Elwin." Ariana scowled at him.

Elwin shrugged. "You would have been too easy on her. She needed to be dropped right into the sea where she could rescue a victim and know that she could withstand the elements and have no fear of the water."

"And the two sharks out there?" Ariana was so exhausted; she couldn't even stand up to punch him.

"Four, but who was counting?"

"No. Way." Juno looked just as angry with Elwin as Ariana was.

"Yep. I sent the video to Catriona already, and she is using it for one of the training videos. Of what to do, and what not to do, I might add. You might have just elevated your position, all because of me." Elwin sounded proud of himself.

"I could kill you." Ariana couldn't believe he'd uploaded a video, well that he'd actually taken the video in the first place and not helped her!

Malik stalked out to join them. "Where the hell were you? We looked everywhere for you. Juno and me. We had no idea where Elwin had gone."

"You should have seen the way she kissed the human she rescued," Elwin said.

Juno raised her brows.

And Ariana was ready to sock Elwin just for that.

CHAPTER 6

*M*alik looked like he was ready to fight someone. Ariana hoped he wasn't mad at *her* for anything. She had nothing to do with any of this! So he'd just better not be angry with her that he hadn't given her the assignment! "Okay, so you said I would have wings when I'm supposed to and not before when here I could have really used them." Thinking of the waves crashing over her, she wondered if her wings *would* have helped her. "But my fae transporting abilities?"

Malik was still frowning at her. "When Catriona believes you're ready to have your abilities, you'll have them."

"I better have gotten credit for this assignment then!"

"That I didn't give you? That nobody gave you?" Malik asked.

She couldn't be more furious with Elwin for putting her through that terror for no good reason, though she had to remind herself, she had saved the human and he was a great kisser!

* * *

MALIK COULDN'T HAVE BEEN MORE furious with Elwin for taking Ariana on a mission that he hadn't given her. Seeing her bedraggled look, he knew that she was telling the truth that she'd been on a sea rescue mission. He pulled a piece of seaweed from her hair. She smelled not of chlorine water cloaking her after a dip in the pool but of the salty sea. And she looked exhausted.

"Are you all right?" he belatedly asked, unable to keep the furor out of his voice. Not with her, but with Elwin.

"Yeah, no thanks to Elwin. He just shoved me into the pool and the next thing I knew, I was in the sea in the middle of a raging storm and trying to rescue a capsized man."

"Wait until you get to the end scene where he kisses her," Elwin said. "I don't think that was supposed to be in the script."

"Why not? I saved him, didn't I?" Ariana sounded just as perturbed with Elwin as much as Malik was.

"I have to admit it looked pretty touch and go. And for your information, I caught the four sharks on the video for you too." Elwin smiled.

* * *

LIKE ELWIN HAD REALLY DONE Ariana a favor!

She shuddered. "I'm going for a swim in a *safe* pool, and don't you dare even think of shoving me in again."

"I think you've gotten over your fear of the water now," Elwin said.

As if! Ariana would have nightmares about this forever!

"Sorry, Ariana. Elwin, you're a piece of work," Juno said. "If it's any consolation to you, Ariana, he threw me off a cliff so I would get over my fear of heights."

"And?" Ariana asked, shocked to the core, though after what he'd done to her, she should have been.

"Thankfully, both my fae transport abilities and wings came to assist me," Juno said.

"And you didn't kill him?" Ariana asked.

"No, but I wanted to. Race you to the pool." Juno cheated, spread her wings, flew over to the center of the pool, made her wings vanish and dropped into the pool.

That's what Ariana wanted to do. "Okay, so I saved two people now." She walked over to the pool and dove in. When she surfaced, she added, "So when do I get some kind of congratulations?"

"Are you kidding? That wasn't your mission," Elwin said, laughing. "Just think you did your good deed for the day."

"You're an idiot," Malik said, and dove into the pool.

"I uploaded the video for anyone who wants to watch it. It really was a harrowing experience. It sure had me on the edge of my seat. I didn't think you and the human would make it," Elwin said.

"Would you have helped me? I mean, him? Since he was the one who needed to be rescued?" Ariana asked.

"Yeah, if you hadn't done the job, since it wasn't your assignment anyway." Elwin smiled.

* * *

"Was he on *any* guardian angel's list to rescue?" Malik asked. There were rules about such a thing. It totally messed up Catriona's schedule when guardian angels went and did their own thing. They weren't allowed to. He didn't think that Ariana would get in trouble for it because Elwin was the one who dumped her into the situation.

"Nope. The guy was at his own peril. No guardian angel had been assigned to him. He was out of luck. Until Ariana miraculously appeared there to save him. Did you tell him you were his guardian angel?" Elwin slipped into the pool to tread water beside them.

"Of course. What use is it being a guardian angel if you can't tell anyone that you are?" Ariana said. "He asked me who I was. So I told him."

"Okay, I just wondered. What did he say?" Elwin asked.

"He laughed. I thought you would have captured that on the video."

The other guardian angels all smiled.

"I must have missed it."

"Typical response from humans and the fae alike," Juno said.

Malik shook his head. "If Ariana gets into trouble for this—"

Just then a runner came looking for both Malik and Ariana. "You have to see Catriona in her office now."

Malik knew they were in trouble. No one violated the rules and got away with it. He should have been looking out for Ariana, but he'd gotten sidetracked when a friend told him he was going to try and jump to the other side—back to the fae world. And when Malik finally was free and headed to the pool, hoping Ariana was still there, she was gone. Juno hadn't had any clue where Ariana was and had even checked Ariana's room and she'd just—vanished. A fae without powers couldn't just vanish, so all the time Malik and Juno had been looking for her, they hadn't even realized Elwin was gone too. Not that it would have meant anything to them.

Elwin could have had a mission, or gone shopping, or whatever it was he liked to do these days. Malik wasn't Elwin's keeper. Malik had tried to fight feeling panicked. Not only because Ariana was his ward, but because he really felt something for her, as much as he didn't want to admit it to himself.

Then to learn she was kissing some human she'd just rescued? He hoped he hadn't turned completely red-faced with irritation over it as hot as his face had suddenly felt. But when he learned Elwin had dropped her in the ocean to face a number of perils to save a human? He was livid. Watch Elwin get away with it too!

Malik took Ariana inside the building and walked her toward Catriona's office.

"I can't believe that Elwin isn't being summoned to Catriona's office and didn't get in trouble for what he did to me though," Ariana said.

"Yeah, I know. He's…special. So he gets away with more stuff than any of the rest of us do."

"So explain to me what this means. Being special."

"I told you. I don't know."

She let out her breath. "Well, I can't fae transport and I don't have wings so I don't feel special at all."

"To me you're special."

"Yeah, so special that—"

He pulled her in for a kiss.

That seemed to have shocked her to pieces! He hadn't planned to do this. Not right away. She really got into the kiss, her hands on his waist, his hands cupping her face. And then they heard someone coming and they quickly separated. Why had he kissed her? Beyond the fact he had been dying to because he didn't want her kissing victims she had to rescue, just him!

* * *

AT CATRIONA'S OFFICE, she motioned for Malik and Ariana to take a seat on the other side of her desk and leaned back in her chair. She had such an imperious expression, he knew he was in trouble.

"I saw the video showing Ariana rescuing the paddler in the sea. Have you seen it?" Catriona asked.

Malik closed his gaping mouth. "Uh, no. Elwin sent Ariana on the sea rescue mission. I had nothing to do with it. Juno and I were going to get her used to getting back in the water in the pool, so Ariana wouldn't hesitate to save someone during a water rescue."

Catriona started the video and it appeared on the white wall where she often showed videos to praise a successful mission, or scold for a failure. Or, in this case, scold for taking on a mission where the human wasn't even supposed to be saved?

"She did a good job, don't you think?" Catriona asked and Malik closed his gaping mouth.

He wasn't sure he would have managed as well as Ariana had, and he had to admit he was proud of her. He admired her resilience in the face of such obstacles and her determination to see it through. He glanced at her, and she was shivering, her own mouth parted in surprise to see what she'd gone through in person, captured for all time. He should have taken her back to her room to allow her to change her clothes first before she met with Catriona. He figured Catriona would use this as a training video of how to save someone in a treacherous sea rescue with a caveat that it was a mistake because she hadn't authorized it.

It took forever for Ariana to rescue the man, one mountain of water rising after another, threatening to thwart her from rescuing him in time. And the sharks! Four of them. Elwin hadn't been fabricating the number when he had mentioned them. Malik was glad she hadn't seen that many sharks or she might have panicked for sure and never finished swimming to the boat.

The man she rescued had blue lips by the time she helped him flip the boat and they both climbed aboard. Blue lips that she warmed up with her own! That should get her a scolding if nothing else.

When the movie ended, Catriona said, "You did well for breaking the rules."

Ariana opened her mouth to object, Malik figured, and he was about to do the same, but Catriona waved her hand to tell them to cease any objection they might be ready to offer. "She clearly is ready to handle advanced rescue missions. Dispense with anything else simple, Malik. Forget the next level and third level of rescue missions. Go straight to the advanced tasks."

Malik stared at Catriona. He couldn't believe she wanted him to give Ariana only the most perilous cases. She needed time to get acclimated. "But—"

"That's all. You're both dismissed."

"Do I get credit for saving the human?" Ariana asked.

Malik knew she shouldn't have bothered asking. Catriona had already said she had broken the rules. She didn't reward such behavior. Didn't Ariana realize moving to advanced rescues was because of that?

Catriona gave her a biting smile, which said it all. No. Way. "Be lucky you're still here with us. Now off with you. I'm sure Malik will have another assignment for you soon."

"And Elwin?" Malik asked.

"He helped prove Ariana doesn't have a fear of the water any longer, didn't he? You were taking baby steps with her when you didn't need to. I told you—she's special."

And dead meat.

"Now, take her out of here. You're both dripping chlorine water all over my leather chair and tile floors." Catriona motioned for them to leave with a wave of her hand.

Malik would have just transported Ariana to her room from Catriona's office, but that wasn't done. So he waited until they were in the hall and he wrapped his arms around her and transported her to her room before she was ready or could object.

"Sorry about what happened to you," Malik said, releasing her. "I will kill Elwin."

"Can you do that?"

"No. But I sure want to. I can't believe he got you into this mess."

She sighed. "Can you leave? I need to shower and change."

"Yeah, sure. Are you ready to watch the videos of how to take care of high-risk rescue missions? Since, thanks to Elwin, that's what you're stuck with now. I could meet you at the viewing room," Malik said.

"Do I need to watch them?"

"Well, if Catriona has anything to say about it, probably no. But since I guess I'm having you take baby steps to make sure you remain safe, then yes, I think it's a wise idea."

"I'll watch them. I feel the same way that you do about Elwin, by the way. He's on my blacklist. See you in a few. I'll just meet you there when I'm done."

"All right." Then Malik left to talk to Elwin and found the fae still hanging around the pool with Juno. Not saying a word, Malik walked up to Elwin and punched him in the eye. Shocked, Elwin and Juno gasped, then Malik stalked off. So much for talking to Elwin. He could have ended Ariana's angel gig before she'd barely gotten started. And Malik would have lost her before he even had a chance to really get to know her.

He went to his room, quickly showered, and changed clothes.

While he waited for her to meet up with him at the viewing room, he pulled the video of Ariana's rescue mission up to watch. Well, fast forward, and when he got to the end where Elwin just had to catch the human and Ariana kissing, Malik edited it out. He allowed the next part where it showed the men rescuing the man and his canoe. The ending was important to show other new angel recruits the follow-up after all was done. To show that the human had actually received help at the end when Ariana's mission was complete.

Malik still couldn't believe that Elwin had done that to her. The more he thought about it, the angrier he got and if Elwin came anywhere near Ariana again, Malik was likely to give him another black eye.

* * *

ARIANA DIDN'T WANT to leave the hot shower as she removed all the chlorine water from her hair and skin. She should have insisted she shower and dress in something else *before* she had to meet with Catriona. She was glad Malik had stuck up for her and didn't want her to have to work on higher level missions right off the bat. She was bound to make more mistakes than if she worked up to the more difficult cases. She felt she'd just gotten really lucky this time. And it didn't even count.

She was just as irritated with Catriona for not giving her credit for saving the human. It wasn't Ariana's fault she'd been put in that position, and she hadn't had any way to return to the angel fae kingdom on her own. She'd had no choice but to save the human.

She wouldn't have done anything differently—even if she'd known he hadn't been on any list of humans who needed to be saved. She supposed that made her an oddity among the fae. She didn't mind playing tricks on the humans, but she didn't want to see them physically hurt, just their pride would do.

She was about to leave her room and join Malik, but when she opened her door, Elwin was standing there, fist raised to knock. He smiled at her, sporting one black eye.

"What happened to you?" she asked, genuinely surprised to see his black eye, but glad someone—she hoped—had given it to him. That he hadn't just stumbled or run into something and injured himself, though that would have amused her also.

"Malik happened to me."

She paused and smiled. She was glad someone had taken action against the fae to prove what he'd done to her wasn't appreciated. "Good. Do that to me again and I'll give you another black eye so you can have a matching pair."

"I did you a favor." Elwin was so arrogant.

"Keep telling yourself that."

"It's true." Elwin began walking with her down to the video room. "Doing the mediocre rescues would have bored you to tears and you would have been asking every fae in the joint how to go about getting out of here."

She grabbed his arm and pulled him to a stop. "You know about it?" Maybe *he* was the one who could tell her how to leave here and return to her normal fae world since he seemed willing to bypass the rules. "Okay, tell me how to get out of here, since you seem to know so much."

Elwin only smiled at her. "Wouldn't you like to know. But that's one thing I wouldn't dare get into trouble over."

"But doing what you did was okay? I don't understand why you didn't get into trouble for that."

"It all has to do with being smarter than the average fae. I did what Malik should have done. Oh, and I caught Malik editing your movie debut." Elwin sounded serious, then offered her a precocious smile, as if he were tarnishing Malik's reputation by spilling the truth so she would be angry with Malik too.

"What?" Ariana asked.

"Yeah, it was my favorite part. Probably yours too. The kiss at the end? Poetic." Elwin saluted her and vanished.

Ariana frowned, then smiled. That was her favorite part of the whole mission too, but she didn't want the whole blasted Angel Corp to witness it. If she'd known it was going to be featured on a video for all to see, she wouldn't have done it. She began walking to the viewing room again. Nah, on second thought, she would have done it. The kiss *had* been her favorite part! Though Malik's kiss was even hotter.

When she reached the viewing room, she found Malik sitting there waiting for her.

"So you didn't like the kissing scene?" she asked.

"What?"

"Elwin said you deleted it."

"He's a jerk. And kissing a rescued victim isn't part of the angel rescue protocol. Since you talked to Elwin, did you tell him what you thought about him for putting you in such a predicament with having to handle much more dangerous cases?"

"He said I would have found the other jobs boring and wanted to leave this place pronto. I asked him about the black eye, and he told me you gave it to him, which he rightly deserved. I told him I would give him a matching one if he pulled anything like that with me again."

Malik smiled at her.

Now, when Malik smiled like that at her, she thought *he* looked even *more* kissable. "Okay, let's see what bad things I have to deal with in the future."

"I hope you're ready for this."

"I guess I'm ready no matter what since Elwin set me up."

"Just think of it this way. If you end up being head angel someday, you can fix him."

She smiled, and she knew it was one of her eviler smiles that said she would do just that.

"Juno's pissed off," Malik said.

"Why?" Ariana asked.

"You got to skip the easy and mid-difficulty cases and shot straight to the difficult ones."

"She can have my job. Seriously. At least she gets to work toward it." Then Ariana frowned. "I thought she'd been here for a long time already."

"She has been. She's only at the mid-level cases."

"And you?"

"Difficult level or Catriona wouldn't have assigned you to me."

Ariana sighed and settled against her seat. "I like Juno. I hope it doesn't sour our beginning friendship. As to Elwin? He's definitely not on my friends' list." She tapped her fingers on the armrest. "Elwin knows how to get out of here."

"What do you mean?"

"How to return to the fae world."

"And you're going to listen to him after what he already pulled with you?"

She shrugged. "Somebody's going to get the nerve up to tell me."

"You don't want to know. Just leave it at that." Then Malik started the movie.

She did too want to know and she was going to learn the truth sooner or later. "Thanks for deleting the kiss scene."

Malik didn't say anything.

"It was too special to show off to the Angel Corp," she added.

* * *

MALIK WANTED to groan out loud. He couldn't believe Ariana was asking Elwin, of all people, how to leave here. From the very beginning, he knew she was going to be trouble. He still couldn't figure out why Catriona thought Ariana was so special, and he was irritated to no end that Catriona didn't punish Elwin, but actually praised him in an offhanded way.

He tried to relax while he watched the videos with Ariana, to answer any questions she might have, but the videos were as harrowing to watch as the mission *she'd* been on, and he hated to think he hadn't been there for her.

She paused the movie, and he was afraid it was too disturbing for her, but she said, "You said you drowned. Why were you at South Padre Island?"

"I loved going to South Padre Island. Just getting away from it all." He didn't want to tell her why he'd been there so much.

"What was your occupation, if you had to get away from it all'?"

"Like you, I was a royal guard, only for the phantom fae."

"No, really?"

"I was." His downfall had been Ariana.

"You never told me what you were watching on the beach that held such fascination for you."

Malik sighed. "*You.* I knew you were a hawk fae and wouldn't have anything to do with me."

"A guardian angel? I guess not."

"No, I hadn't died yet."

"You were watching me? When?"

That's what he had suspected. No matter how many times he had chanced to see her, she had never seen him. "Several times when you would come to the beach with your friend. I liked the beach and the ocean. And I especially liked it when you were there. You never were with a guy, and you didn't flirt with the human males like your friend did." Malik shrugged. "I thought I might have a chance to…talk to you sometime. Then I drowned."

"And were eaten by a shark."

He smiled. That was his favorite part of the story, though he didn't tell everyone the truth. His friends who had been royal guards like him loved to hear his tales when they weren't busy on duty, though sometimes even when they were. It made the dull nights pass more quickly and kept them all awake on the job. He was even known to tell a story or two while fighting a battle with the enemy. It somehow gave him the advantage as they thought he was addled when he was anything but. He did very well at multitasking.

"Okay, wait. Everyone who is here saved someone when they died. If the boat capsized and struck you and you drowned, how did you save anyone?" Ariana asked.

CHAPTER 7

$\mathcal{M}$ alik was hopeful Ariana would do all right with harder cases when she hadn't been given the opportunity to work up to them. He couldn't believe Catriona would think she was ready. Sure, Ariana did fine on an unplanned rescue, but she hadn't even gotten credit for it! He didn't think that was fair to her at all.

She'd only managed to handle one authorized simple rescue and he really felt that wasn't enough.

Now he was bringing the first sanctioned, possibly dangerous mission to her that she'd have to deal with, and he knocked on Ariana's door late that night. That was the thing about being in the Angel Corp. They never knew when they would have to go on a mission. People didn't only need guardian angels during the day.

When he knocked on the door to Ariana's room, she didn't respond. He knocked again. Man, she was a heavy sleeper. He knocked a third time and she snapped, "What? *Go. Away.*"

He smiled. She was not a night owl. "I have a mission for you." He continued to stand at the door, waiting and waiting and waiting. He frowned. She better not have gone back to sleep and instead was getting dressed in a hurry. He knocked again. "Ariana! Catriona gave me a mission for you to take care of. Now."

Ariana finally opened the door, her eyes half closed, frowning at him. "What? Do you know what time of night it is?"

"Two in the morning. Hey, if I wasn't your mentor, I wouldn't have been awakened to bring this to you and I could have been sleeping my night away." Unless he'd had a mission of his own, but while being Ariana's mentor, he wouldn't.

She was still wearing pajamas.

"You have to get dressed quickly. We need to go like before, when I first knocked on your door."

"I thought you were a nightmare. Well, I still do." She shut the door in his face, and he hoped that meant she was going to dress.

A few minutes later, she opened the door. "Okay, so who have I got to save this time?"

Malik showed her a picture. "There. That man."

* * *

"WHAT? You've got to be kidding me." This time it wasn't a human Ariana was supposed to save, but a fae.

"I'm not joking about this. Why would I?" Malik asked, sounding totally serious.

"No way. Duke Tully? He abducts royal or wealthy fae and releases them only after someone pays him a substantial ransom. And he doesn't rob to give to the poor. I doubt that he's ever done a kindness in his life."

"That's the mission. And right now he has a hostage in Kingwood Forest."

Ariana frowned as she studied the handsome duke in the photo. She knew he never harmed his hostages, but she felt he was not someone who was worth saving either. "How difficult is this going to be?"

"The fae, in general, do not believe in angels. The same with many humans. So all assignments tend to be tough. Come on, let's go. I'm sure the duke will be a challenge. He listens to no one."

No kidding. Ariana swore Catriona was giving her a no-win case just to see her fail. At least Malik was going to be with her. Recording the case, probably, but maybe this time he'd feel sorry for her and help her out if she needed him to since it could be a dangerous mission.

"Oh, and Catriona gave you your wings and your transporting abilities back, just so you'd be able to manage the more difficult cases."

"Well, *finally*." She didn't even have time to display her wings to see them when Malik grabbed her arm, startling her, and whisked her away.

* * *

WHEN ARIANA and Malik arrived at the camp of Duke Tully in Kingwood Forest, he'd already taken a princess and her lady-in-waiting hostage. Ariana was shocked to see the princess was Esmeralda, the hawk fae princess. She was the sister of King Tiernan, the hawk fae king, whom Ariana had worked for as a guard for the royal family. How had the royal guard allowed this to happen?

If Ariana had been there still protecting them, Esmeralda would have been home, safe and sound, guaranteed.

Ariana walked through the camp, and no one was seeing her, as it should be. As a fae, she couldn't be invisible to the fae. But as an angel, no one spied her unless she allowed it. Which was kind of cool. Except, to her surprise, the princess. Esmeralda's green eyes were wide as she stared at her. Esmeralda smiled at Ariana, then quickly lost the smile and glanced around the campfire, appearing afraid someone else might see Ariana. So what did it mean? That Esmeralda was surprised to see Ariana alive? Or that she knew she was dead, and she had to be a ghost? At least now, Ariana could ask her what had happened back home.

Why couldn't Ariana be there to save the princess instead?

She decided she would be. At least she could do some good before she had to save the annoying duke. Ariana walked straight up to Esmeralda and smiled. "You see me."

"Yes. You've been sent to free me," the princess whispered.

Then Ariana saw Malik lurking in the woods nearby. She realized she didn't want him to see her avoiding what she was supposed to be doing. Then again, she didn't see that the duke was in any kind of life-threatening danger. He was just eating by the fire with his men, drinking ale, having a great time of it.

"Can you retire to bed?" Ariana asked the princess.

"I will take my leave," Esmeralda said to the duke as she rose to her feet, a little stiffly.

"Take her to her tent," the duke ordered, and a man hurried to do his bidding.

Ariana joined Esmeralda in the tent and immediately, Esmeralda whispered, "We thought you were dead. I didn't know you could hide your fae aura."

"I can't." But that meant Esmeralda thought Ariana was still alive. Still, how did Esmeralda see her at all when no one else could? "Okay, look, I'm going to get you out of here." Ariana planned to just transport her to the hawk fae kingdom, though it was too far to travel. She would have to take her to one of the closer kingdoms that had alliances with the hawk fae.

Then Malik walked into the tent and Esmeralda gasped. "You have a friend to help you, Ariana?"

He straightened his back, looking all imperious. "Ariana has another mission to do. And spiriting you away isn't on the agenda."

But it was. Okay, so maybe Ariana could save the duke first, and then take Esmeralda home.

Esmeralda tilted her chin up. "She works for my brother, King Tiernan, as one of the royal guards. This is too her mission."

"How is it that you see us?" Malik asked, displaying his wings.

Ariana could have hit him.

Esmeralda covered her mouth to silence a scream.

"Do you want all the guards to come in here?" Ariana asked, furious with him.

"Saving the princess isn't your job, Ariana."

"Do you want to date me or not?" Ariana asked Malik. There. She said it. Maybe angels didn't date, but if he let her have her way, she'd date him. After all, an angel who would help her be a rebel and aid others who really needed her help couldn't be all that bad.

Malik closed his gaping mouth. Then he cast her a little smirk. Okay, so was he going for it or not?

"All right, but we have to save...I mean, you have to save the duke first," Malik said.

"Why?" both Esmeralda and Ariana said at the same time.

Ariana was a little wary of Malik for accepting the quest so easily. Would she be whisked back to the angel plane of existence once she completed her task of saving the duke and then she wouldn't be able to save Esmeralda?

"Because if you don't, you will be in big trouble." Malik looked so cross at her, she wanted to laugh, but she stifled the urge.

"I'll take her to the dragon fae kingdom. They can alert the hawk fae and take her home or let them come for her. They have an alliance with the hawk fae," Ariana said. "When is Duke Tully supposed to be in danger? And what kind of harm was supposed to befall him?" She could imagine he'd made many an enemy with taking royals hostage for ransom.

"We never know that for sure. When we see what might look like danger, we can assume it—like the kids bungee jumping off the bridge where danger signs had been posted and the girl with the ball and the pool. In cases like this, we really don't know, and we have to be vigilant at all times," Malik said.

"Okay, so you watch the duke and if he gets into trouble, you cover for me."

Malik shook his head.

"All right." As much as she wanted to take Esmeralda safely to the dragon fae kingdom herself, she said to Malik, "I'll stay here, and you take the princess there."

"I'm your mentor. I have to stay with you at all times to—"

"Record my progress?"

He let out his breath in exasperation. "All right. I'll take her. Don't get yourself into trouble in the meantime or it's on both our heads."

Ariana crossed the tent and gave him a hug, but he wasn't willing to let her go without a kiss—to seal the bargain with her. He was a *really* great kisser, so she was perfectly all right with the arrangement. Well, except she still wished she could take Esmeralda herself.

She gave Esmeralda a hug next. But the princess was staring at her, looking shocked to her very soul. "You're...you're both...angels?"

"Uh, yes, but I'm going to find my way home as soon as I can." Ariana tried to summon her wings, and there they were, bold as day, bright and white and feathery and beautiful.

"Oh," Esmeralda gasped.

"Beautiful," Malik said.

Ariana wondered when she lost her wings once she returned to the fae world for good would he be as interested in her? She'd be a hawk fae again then. Maybe.

"Is there anything here you want to take with you?" Ariana asked the princess.

"My lady-in-waiting! Lady Winnie!" Esmeralda called out, as if she'd nearly forgotten her in her excitement to see Ariana.

The woman hurried into the tent, but she didn't seem to see either of the angels standing inside.

"This is going to be a problem," Malik said.

"We both have to take one of them." Esmeralda motioned to the fae irons on Esmeralda and her lady-in-waiting's ankles. They couldn't fae transport themselves. The angels would have to transport them to the dragon fae kingdom.

"Take Winnie first," Esmeralda implored.

"No. You're the one being ransomed," Malik said. "Ariana, you stay here and save the duke. I'll return for the maid after I leave Esmeralda off with the dragon fae."

"Thank you, Malik."

"Who are you talking to?" Winnie asked Esmeralda.

"My guardian angels." Then Esmeralda smiled and Malik shook his head at Ariana.

"Do your duty, Ariana," he ordered, and then he took Esmeralda in his arms, and for a second, Ariana felt a tinge of jealousy that he was holding her close, and that was ludicrous.

"Where, how...," Winnie said.

Ariana appeared before the maid as an angel with her wings spread out, and the woman looked at her and fainted dead away. Well, that worked for Ariana. Now she had to locate that pesky duke and keep him safe, against her better judgement.

* * *

MALIK WAS BERATING himself the whole time he was headed to the dragon fae kingdom with the princess. He shouldn't have allowed Ariana to talk him into leaving her. He had to fly with his angel wings instead of transporting from the forest because the distance was too great.

"What did everyone have to say of Ariana's disappearance?" Malik had to ask Esmeralda because he knew Ariana would want to know and he was curious about it too, being a, well, former fae.

"Shocked that she had drowned. We can easily transport ourselves away from danger, usually, unless it's in the heat of battle, or we are clamped in irons. When her friend, Charity, returned home without her, she told us what had happened, that Ariana had drowned while trying to save human girls and had actually saved both of them. Everyone was shocked and sorry to hear the news. But she was celebrated for the hero she was."

"How is it that you can see us?"

"I have always been able to see angels. I'm surprised she would be sent to help the duke though. I didn't realize she was an angel at first, thinking she hadn't drowned since no one had found a body, and here she was, doing her duty, coming to protect me."

"I'm sorry she couldn't bring you to safety. I don't want her to be in trouble for disobeying her Angel Corp directive."

"What about you?"

"I'm her mentor, so yeah, if she messes up, I'll be in trouble too."

"I can't thank you enough for helping us. And I know she would have taken me home if she could have. She's the most unselfish fae I've ever known. You got something out of the bargain I guess too."

Malik smiled. "Yeah." Despite his not saving Ariana when he was supposed to, she seemed to honestly like him and he was over the moon for that.

When he finally reached the wall walk of the dragon fae kingdom, he alighted and set Esmeralda on her feet. "I must leave at once to bring your lady-in-waiting here before Ariana finds herself in trouble. And your maid as well."

Dragon fae guards were racing toward the two of them and Malik showed his wings in all his angelic glory. That had the guards stopping in their tracks.

"Angel Malik has rescued me from the Kingwood Forest and he's off to rescue my lady-in-waiting from Duke Tully. I'm Princess Esmeralda."

"I know you, my lady. I'm Halloran, Dragon at Arms, in charge of all the dragon fae royal guards. If Malik knows where the duke is camped, we will rescue your lady, and take care of Duke Tully as well." Halloran gave her an evil smile.

Now Malik was worried. What if the dragons meant to kill Duke Tully and Ariana was in the middle of it, trying to save him? And Malik was the one who had initiated the whole thing by bringing Esmeralda here for safekeeping, putting Ariana in this position? *Great.* When it came to her, he swore he just couldn't think clearly, and everything went awry.

Halloran and a team of ten of his dragon friends, including his sister, Ena, all came with him to help.

This could be a disaster.

CHAPTER 8

*A*riana was torn between staying with Winnie, Princess
Esmeralda's lady-in-waiting, to ensure her safety should
anyone learn the princess had vanished and sticking with the
duke to do her job. She didn't know how long it would take for
Malik to deliver Esmeralda and return. A long time, she was
afraid. If she hadn't been worried about Winnie's safety, Ariana
could just move her from camp to the woods farther away from
here. But then she would be concerned something else might
happen to Winnie.

Winnie woke from her faint before Ariana could leave the
tent and knew she had to change plans and talk to the maid first.
"Come on, Winnie. We'll make it look like the princess is sleeping. Then you lie down on your mat. Malik will be back before
you know it."

"You're…you're dead. They said you were dead. That you had
drowned."

"We'll take care of you. I promise." Ariana didn't want to
explain the whole angel business with her. She was tired and she
needed to get some sleep if she was to protect the duke.

Winnie was wringing her hands, and then she nodded, and

they made the makeshift princess in her bed. Then Winnie laid down on her own mat.

"Scream if anyone tries to harm you or you have any trouble at all." Because Ariana was going to protect the lady no matter what.

Winnie nodded vigorously, her eyes wide.

No longer visible to anyone, Ariana headed out of the tent, looking for the man she was supposed to protect, whom she didn't want to protect.

When she found him, he was just joking with some of his men around one of the campfires. He didn't seem to be in any danger whatsoever. She sighed. Had Catriona been mistaken about all this?

Then Ariana realized she hadn't asked Esmeralda how her father had taken the news about her death. How her friends or anyone else had either, for that matter. She would do anything to see them again. To let them know she was okay. Well, she'd be even better off if she could return to her home as a fae.

"I'm going to be back in a minute," Duke Tully said to his men.

Two of his men were going with him and Ariana figured he had enough guards to protect him. She suspected he was going to relieve himself in the woods, which she didn't want to witness. She hoped that wasn't a part of a guardian angel's duty.

She watched the woods though, listening to the sounds of an owl off in the distance, the bugs making a racket, the men in camp laughing and talking still.

Tully and his men finally returned to camp and then after he made sure everyone who was supposed to be on guard duty was, he retired to his tent.

Ariana never understood why a duke, who owned a castle and land, would be running around in the woods taking royal hostages as if he was so bored with life, he had nothing better to do with it.

She wanted to retire to the princess's tent and take her place on the bedding to sleep, and to watch out for Winnie, but she figured she was supposed to stay with the duke, as much as she didn't like the idea.

For a while, Ariana stood outside his noble, red and gold tent, flags flying in the breeze. He was proud of who he was. She was surprised no one had found him before and thrown him in a dungeon. Then she sat down outside the tent, but it was beginning to get cold out there, a nippy breeze sweeping around her face. She rose to her feet and peered into the tent. Duke Tully was sound asleep, dreaming of the gold he would get from King Tiernan for Princess Esmeralda's release, no doubt. Not this time. She smiled at the thought that she had thwarted him on his mission.

She paced inside his square tent, the canvas ceiling high enough for his tall stature even. Annoyed he was lying comfortably underneath a feathered quilt, she wondered if he'd notice if she took it from him. She slipped it carefully off him and wrapped it around herself. He still had a couple of more blankets for himself. Curling up on the canvas floor, she fell fast asleep.

Until she heard two sounds—Duke Tully cursing that someone had stolen his quilt and the flapping of several dragons' wings heading in the direction of the camp.

Ohmigoddess! Malik hadn't returned just for Winnie. He'd brought a fleet of dragons and they were sure to kill Duke Tully for this outrage. What had Malik been thinking? Was this how she was supposed to save the duke? By fighting a dozen dragons?

Forget that! Tully apparently heard the dragons too and was hurrying to dress. "Break camp!" he shouted, practically in her ear.

She dropped the quilt and the only thing that came to mind in her panic—it was Catriona's fault she hadn't allowed Ariana more training time before she took on missions like this—was to transport the duke somewhere safe.

She grabbed Tully in her arms. He cried out because she

hadn't made herself visible to him and she smiled. It was high time someone scared *him*! She transported home. Not her real home. But to the one in the clouds that she was now stuck at on the angel plane.

She just hoped Malik wouldn't get into any trouble over this.

When she arrived, she hadn't anticipated where she'd land, and she and Duke Tully ended up in the swimming pool near the stairs. Elwin was floating on a shark float, and she'd startled him so, he fell off it into the water. *Good.* He deserved it.

She realized here it was daytime, not in the middle of the night.

"What have you done?" Juno asked, running out to see Ariana with Duke Tully in the water, climbing up the stairs to leave the pool.

"My mission. I accomplished it," Ariana said brightly.

Elwin climbed back on top of his float. "You-know-who isn't going to be happy about this." Then he frowned and looked around. "Where's Malik?"

Safe, she hoped.

Duke Tully was looking all around the place, glancing at them, trying to figure out what was going on, Ariana figured, as she dragged him out of the water. Now he was *her* hostage. How did he like that?

"Who are you people?" Duke Tully asked. "Where am I?"

"You're where you can't take anyone hostage," Ariana said, wishing she could just leave him here.

"Oh, oh, I know who he is. Duke Tully," Juno said. "You had to save *him*?" She was frowning, looking the same way as Ariana had felt about saving someone so unworthy. "Where are you taking him? You can't keep him here."

Elwin smiled. "Sure. Keep him here. I'd love to see Catriona's reaction when she learns of it."

Ariana just figured he would.

* * *

THE DRAGONS quickly rounded up as many of Duke Tully's men as they could find, some of them scattered in the surrounding woods as Malik helped them, though he'd been searching for Ariana specifically.

Ena said, "I'll take Winnie to the castle."

"Some of our dragons will go with you, but where is Duke Tully?" Halloran asked.

Malik had wanted to warn Ariana in the worst way about the trouble coming for them, worried she might try to fight the dragons to protect him because it was her mission, nothing more, but she must have taken Duke Tully away. But to where?

Once Malik helped Halloran and the others search for Duke Tully to no avail, Halloran and his dragons thanked him and headed for home.

Malik just stared at the campsite trampled by the dragons, the campfires all out. He had no idea where Ariana might have taken Tully. But if this had been the reason Tully's life had been in danger, Ariana had accomplished her mission.

Still, Malik was also the reason for the duke being in danger in the first place and ultimately, Ariana having to do this mission.

He should have told Ariana if they ever became separated on a mission, well, then what? The truth was she had to stay with her subject to protect him or her. Malik had no clue where she had gone and he finally gave up and returned home, thinking afterward she might have returned to the hawk fae territory to see her family. But the travel would take too long, and she'd have to stay at one of the other castles instead and any of the people there might very well have tossed the duke in their dungeon if she'd taken him with her. Unless she took him back to his own castle. No one had a clue where it was though.

When Malik arrived back at the angel realm, he sure hoped he wasn't mistaken in coming here first. He went to her room, but she didn't answer his knock at the door. Then he went to the swimming pool area to see if anyone was out there and had seen Ariana. He saw Juno talking to a girlfriend and she waved at him and hurried to end her conversation to join him.

"Where in the world have you been? I thought you had the job of mentoring Ariana for the time-being." Juno sounded highly annoyed with him.

He suspected from Juno's question that Ariana had to have been here. "I do have the job of watching over her. We got separated."

"Wow. How in the world did you manage that? She caused all kinds of havoc here," Juno said.

That's what he was afraid of. That she had returned without Malik, and everyone was shocked about it. "Where is she?" This was all Malik's fault, and he should have realized she would have gotten herself into a bind without him staying by her side the whole time to guide her.

"She left already. No one ever brings a living fae here," Juno said.

Malik's jaw dropped. "She brought Duke Tully here?" He would never hear the end of it from Catriona. Or from anyone else for that matter. He never thought she'd bring a living fae here, but she'd never been told not to either. He thought she had just returned here without the duke.

Then Malik saw Elwin on his way to intercept them, a smug, knowing look on his face. Malik didn't need his commentary right now.

"If Juno didn't tell you already, Ariana left. She didn't tell us where she was going, though Duke Tully was pleading with her to give him another chance at a do-over if she'd take him to his own castle."

"Do you believe that?" Juno asked Elwin.

"Nope."

Neither did Malik. "Did she appear inclined to believe the duke and take him to his castle?"

"Who knows? I don't know if she's that gullible or not," Juno said.

"Thanks." Since Malik didn't have any other leads, he might as well check out that one. He left then, transporting to the fae world, and flying as an angel to where he had heard rumors that the duke's castle was hidden in Kingwood Forest. It was said that Duke Tully had paid a magic user to cast a spell over the entire castle and no fae, except for the duke, could see it. As an angel, could Malik detect it? He wasn't sure, but he sincerely hoped so. More than anything, he hoped Ariana was safe and not in any danger.

Yeah, sure, they were angels, but he still was afraid of what might happen to her.

He walked for an hour through Kingwood Forest and realized he had no idea where he was going, and he wasn't getting any vibes that the castle could be here. So much for being able to use angel detection for hidden magical objects. Feeling horribly frustrated and worried for Ariana, he thought about Ena's mate, Brett, who was a dragon and capable of a great deal of magic. Would he be able to detect a magically hidden castle? He'd known Brett when he'd been taken hostage by the phantom fae. Brett had been raised as a human before that, and Ena had thought he was a fae seer—a human who could see the fae's aura. To both their surprise, it turned out he was a phantom fae mage who had to be trained. But he was also the grandson of Prince Sol, the sun dragon. Brett had only been a human, so everyone had thought, but he was a prince among the dragon fae, and in marrying Ena, she had become a princess when all along she had only been a warrior dragon. Though at one point, Queen Irenis of the dark fae had made her a duchess.

The other option was that Ariana had taken Tully to her hawk fae kingdom, but that would be too far to transport to, and he didn't think anyone would house the duke, unless they put him in the dungeon. Maybe that's what Ariana was supposed to do though. Take him to a castle where he'd be incarcerated, and no one would terminate him then. Malik just didn't know what to think. The angels never knew what happened to the people they saved long-term. Or what made them special enough to save. That was beyond their need to know.

He just had to find Ariana—mostly because he cared about her and he was worried for her, but also because he knew before long, Catriona would wonder what had happened to the two of them.

He took off for Ena and Brett's castle and when he arrived there, he had a warm welcome. But he was so concerned about Ariana, he couldn't quit thinking about it. "Hey, sorry to barge in on you, but I can't find Ariana."

"The hawk fae's former royal guard," Ena said, welcoming him in to sit in their great hall.

"She was on an angel mission to save Duke Tully," Malik admitted. "We didn't know how he was in danger, but then when I returned to take Winnie to safety, all of you came with me and Ariana had to move him from the campsite to keep him safe."

Brett let out his breath. "Why didn't you tell us that to begin with? We wouldn't have had to spend all that time searching for him."

"You captured several of his other men," Malik reminded Brett.

"True. But Halloran was determined to find him, and Duke Tully has no trouble replacing his lost men with others eager to live on the edge who want to make some coin at it. So why are you here then?" Brett asked.

"You're a magic user."

Brett raised his brows in question.

"Okay, listen. I don't know where Ariana is. I'm worried about her. I don't care anything about Tully. But I do care about Ariana accomplishing her missions and then returning safely to her new home before our boss learns she's missing."

"And how does my knowing about magic have anything to do with anything?" Brett asked, sitting back against his chair.

"I'm wondering if the duke convinced her to go to his castle and leave him there. What if he incarcerated her there? She hasn't returned to the angel realm again and going to the hawk fae kingdom isn't an option. It's too far and it would take her too long. She would have to stay somewhere else in the interim. And if she still is in charge of Duke Tully, she won't want him to be incarcerated, concerned that would go against what she's supposed to do with him."

"Tully's castle is hidden by magic, it is said," Brett said.

"Yeah, I know. And I can't find it. Can you?"

"No, or Halloran and others would have asked my assistance in finding it long ago. Whoever hid the castle is the only one who could reveal it to others," Brett said.

"What about Duke Tully's men? Wouldn't they have to know where it is?" Malik ran his hands through his hair. Ariana was sure to get another mission and neither of them would be there to accept it. Not to mention he had failed to record how Ariana had saved Duke Tully's life in the first place.

"Most likely Tully would know that and would have it set up that he is the only one who can see it and then let others into the castle. Otherwise, like in a situation like this where some of his men are imprisoned, they could be forced to tell their captors where the castle is. Though even if they mentioned the area, some magic users can make a portal to the castle and those allowed to use it could enter it from different locations so we'd never know where it was truly located," Brett said. "That's how I would do it if I were to hide a castle."

"He can't hurt Ariana, can he?" Ena asked.

"If he had his magic user lock her up in his castle maybe,"

Brett said, then shook his head. "I don't know. You're the first angel I've ever met. What do you think, Malik?"

"I don't know," Malik said, not sure if a magic user's spells could bind a guardian angel to the fae world.

Ena glanced at Brett. "Are you sure you can't do anything to help locate and free Ariana?" Ena was used to taking on dangerous missions and getting paid handsomely for it, so Malik knew she was always eager to help—even in a situation like this where she wouldn't get paid.

Brett reached over and patted Ena's leg and Malik hoped that was a yes.

CHAPTER 9

*A*riana wasn't gullible. At least she never thought of herself in that way. Until now. When Duke Tully convinced her that since she was his guardian angel and he would only be safe at his castle, she figured that's just what she was supposed to do—to take him there. She didn't know where else to take him where he would be safe and since that was her job, she had agreed. She really needed to get rid of him and rejoin Malik before they both got into trouble, more so than she was afraid she might be after taking Tully to the angel realm. What did she know?

"Take me to the northeast corner of Kingwood Forest," Tully directed her.

She didn't remember ever coming across any castle in that location. "Are you sure?" Though she realized how silly that sounded when she figured he would have to know exactly where he had left his castle.

They landed in the area of the forest that he had said the castle would be located in and then they walked a short distance through the pine trees. There wasn't any sign of a castle, just trails leading through the woods. Nothing else. She desperately wanted to ask him if he knew where he was going.

Then suddenly it was there. A moat filled with water, a drawbridge with the bridge down, double wooden doors closed to the public, a wall surrounding the castle, round towers at the four corners, and a wall walk around the top, connecting them. No one seemed to be guarding the place. A mist rose from the water, the cool air mixing with the warm water, making it appear ghostly. The duke's flags flying above the towers, swept back and forth in the stiff breeze.

Ariana said, "Okay, well, I delivered you here and now I have to go." When she tried to leave, she realized she couldn't transport herself. What in the world was going on? Had Catriona removed her ability to transport because of what she'd done by bringing the duke to the angel realm?

Ariana tried to make her wings appear, planning to just fly away and hopefully return to her room so she could slip away and get some sleep, though she needed to leave Malik a note to tell him she was home. But she couldn't! Her wings were gone like she'd never had them in the beginning. She couldn't believe that Catriona would keep her there when Ariana needed to get back if she wanted any more work out of her!

Okay, fine. She'd just walk to the first kingdom she could reach, one where the occupants wouldn't mind her visiting them for an overnight stay or two. Somehow, she had to get word to Malik so he could take her home and she'd try to square this with Catriona. But then she worried, what if Catriona had taken away *his* ability to transport and taken away *his* wings too?

"Come on. It's time to eat breakfast. Thanks for saving my life. You can still eat, right?" Duke Tully asked her.

Ariana hesitated to answer him. Yeah, and she was hungry, but she didn't want to stay here.

"Thanks, I'll pass." Then she turned and walked off, but she saw the castle drawbridge in front of her...again. When it should have been behind her. Ahead of her should have been the forest. Frowning, she turned to see the duke waving his hand at the doors to the courtyard and they opened.

And then he walked inside, turned, and said, "Coming?"

She looked behind her and the castle was there too. Oh, just terrific. This all had to do with magic. Would anyone even find her here? Would the angels be able to see through the magic surrounding the duke's castle?

It looked like the duke had put her on an unscheduled vacation from guardian angel duty. But what she realized was—he had taken *her* hostage! If Catriona learned the truth, would she change her mind about having had Ariana serve as the duke's guardian angel?

She just couldn't believe this. And poor Malik. He had only done her bidding because she had told him he could be her boyfriend. She had been serious about it too, but she hadn't meant to get him into any trouble over it. She just figured they'd get the princess and her lady to safety, and she'd take care of the duke. Here he'd been totally deceitful with her when she had saved his life!

She followed him to the castle doors and then walked inside. "Where are your guards?"

"No need to have them."

In the inner baily, the story was different. The castle courtyard was filled with people doing morning chores: feeding chickens, cows, pigs, exercising horses, practicing swordsmanship, washing clothes.

"Do you come here often?" she asked, wondering when he would leave here again and hoping he'd take her with him so she could make her escape.

"Sure. I'm only out and about when I need to stretch my legs."

"To take a royal hostage."

"You know, they're not out on the roads all the time. Only occasionally."

"Lucky for them."

Then he escorted her inside the castle and to a great hall where the food was being set out on long tables. The aroma of wild boar permeated the air, making her stomach growl.

"My lord, we didn't know you would be returning so soon." An older man with gray hair and slate blue eyes wearing a rich silk tunic and suede pants greeted him and then studied Ariana.

So he could see her when she thought she was cloaking her angel persona?

"This is…" Duke Tully glanced at Ariana. "Forgive me. I don't know your name."

"Ariana."

"Ariana, my guardian angel, Baron Bahira. Ariana, Bahira is my devoted advisor."

The old man smiled. She got the impression he thought she was the duke's girlfriend. *Please.*

Then the duke had her sit beside him at the high table, his courtiers all taking their seats to break their fast.

"Why don't you have a duchess?" Ariana asked the duke, curious.

"When the time is right, I will."

"You would have to give up your hostage-taking ways," Ariana guessed.

"Or find a maid who goes along with what I do for a living. Though in truth, I have all that I want anyway. If I didn't get so seasick, I would have been a pirate or a privateer."

Ariana shook her head. Then she saw a man enter the great hall and everyone stopped talking to turn and see him make his entrance. She suspected he must be someone of importance or no one would have noticed or reacted.

"Come, Faraday, we have a special guest. This is Ariana, my guardian angel," Duke Tully said, motioning for him to join them.

The blond-haired man wasn't wearing anything special. Just the typical tunic of leather and breeches of cotton, his boots a brown suede. His blue eyes took in everything though, and her especially. He cast her a hint of a smile and she didn't like the gleam in his eye. Like he knew just what she was, and they could use that to their advantage.

What? Did they think they could ransom her to the Angel Corp? More likely Catriona would send Ariana away in a puff of mist or whatever became of angels who screwed up their missions. She would *not* pay a ransom for one unruly angel.

Faraday joined the duke, Ariana, and Bahira at the head table. Some other men and women were sitting there as well, mostly intrigued about the woman the duke was calling his guardian angel. Faraday probably didn't believe she truly was.

If nothing else, though Ariana was fit to be tied that she couldn't seem to just leave this place, she'd never been given the honor of sitting up at the head table—even when she had saved the king and queen's lives—at any royal feast, and so that was something she hadn't expected.

"After the meal, I would offer to take you on a hunt, but I think that's not really prudent right now," the duke said.

"Why?" Because he would have to take her out into the woods, and she could escape the magic enchantment of the castle?

He smiled.

"What do you intend to do with her?" Faraday asked.

"She is beyond priceless. My very own guardian angel," Tully said.

Great. That's what she'd been afraid of. *"Catriona, if you're listening, you'd better do something about this guy."*

"You can't keep me here. I was given the one job to save you. It's done. I need to protect others who need me to save them," she said, buttering a slice of bread. Other lives could be at stake because the duke was holding her hostage here. She realized just how selfish he was.

"Whoever is in charge will send someone else. No one will miss you, I'm sure," Tully said, as if she were only important to him.

She glanced at Faraday. "Are you the wizard who cast the spell over this castle?"

Faraday smiled and inclined his head. "I am one and the same and honored to meet my first guardian angel."

So he did know she was truly one. "How come your spell affects me like it does? I wouldn't think you could cast a spell that would make an angel lose her abilities to transport, or to show off her wings, or—"

"To be visible to others? I didn't think it would happen either. But here you are, and you don't seem to be able to go anywhere. I think I deserve some compensation for that, don't you, Duke Tully?" Faraday asked.

Duke Tully looked a little surprised to think his wizard would want more for keeping her here.

But she assumed that the wizard was being serious about it, though he hadn't done anything extra to make this happen. She figured with a snap of his fingers he could make this all go away and suddenly the duke's castle would be exposed to the whole fae world.

She realized just how much the wizard had control over Duke Tully's domain. Served the duke right for employing a wizard to do his bidding. Though King Tiernan had his own wizard, he didn't use him for subterfuge. But many of the kingdoms had their own wizards and that evened the playing field if any of the rulers used them in combat between the regions.

Faraday raised a brow, waiting for Tully's response. The duke gave him a small smile. "Sure. What would you like?"

"The angel."

Ariana choked on the sip of the honeyed mead she'd just taken.

"Something else," the duke said dryly.

Right. Anything else. She didn't want to be a pawn of a wizard. She could imagine what a disaster that would be. Well, more so than things were right now.

"I will have to think on it," Faraday said. She didn't like the sinister way he looked at her.

"I take it you aren't going to put me in the dungeon following the meal," Ariana said to Tully, wanting to change the topic in a hurry.

Duke Tully smiled. "You are free to roam the castle and its grounds. You won't be confined to any place."

"Except to the castle and its grounds."

"Precisely. You will want for nothing."

Her freedom, but he knew that. "Okay, so you want to keep me here as your guardian angel, right? But I've lost my ability to protect you."

"Aye, but you are still unique. What other fae can say they have the beautiful company of a guardian angel all his own? Besides, I owe you for saving my life."

"And this is how you repay me?" He truly was a scoundrel.

"You may enjoy anything we have to offer here. You'll be treated as though you were my duchess."

She frowned at him. Oh, joy.

"What kind of fae were you before you became an angel?"

"Hawk fae, a royal bodyguard for Queen Ritasia and King Tiernan."

Duke Tully's eyes widened. "You knew Princess Esmeralda then."

"Yes. And I thought…" She was going to say he was despicable for taking her hostage. Princess Esmeralda had been held hostage by the griffin fae for many years. Ariana couldn't imagine how awful Esmeralda had to have felt that yet another fae had taken her hostage and confined her against her will.

Everyone at the head table waited for Ariana to finish what

she had to say, and she realized she was a prisoner and was in the duke's good graces for the moment. She was here at his whim to do with as he pleased.

She changed her mind about what she was going to say and said instead, "You know Princess Esmeralda had been a hostage of the griffin fae for many years."

"Aye, so she is used to it."

Ariana wanted to slap the silly smirk off the duke's face. No one would ever get "used" to being taken hostage. "Do you mind if I lay down? I've been up all night and I'm so tired, I can barely stay awake." She wasn't lying either. The food was great, the wild boar, the pickled potatoes, the garden greens, even the freshly baked bread. But she could barely keep her eyes open. "I can barely think straight."

"To attempt an escape plot?"

"To carry on a worthwhile conversation." Even though she knew that she wasn't supposed to leave a meal until the head honcho left at royal functions, she just couldn't manage to stay awake, and she was afraid her head would be resting in her plate before long.

The duke motioned to one of his maids. When she joined them, he said, "Take the lady to the women's wing to the best suite we have available. She wishes to rest. Make sure she has clothes and anything else she might need to make her comfortable. Prepare a bath for her if she'd like. You can accompany her to show her the castle and the grounds, but if she prefers to walk alone, she may."

"Aye, my lord. My lady?" The pleasing woman wasn't much older than Ariana, her black hair braided and swept up in a bun, her dark brown eyes kindly. She looked a little awed to have this assignment.

Ariana rose from her seat and as soon as she took her first step, she stumbled. She wasn't exaggerating about being tired.

She didn't do well in any capacity—bodyguard or guardian angel, if she didn't get her well-deserved eight hours of sleep.

Faraday was on his feet in an instant, catching her arm to steady her, looking as though he hadn't given up the notion that she would be his prize instead of Duke Tully's. "Do you wish me to carry you above stairs?"

"No, thanks, I'll be fine."

Then she left with the maid. "I'm Ariana. What's your name?"

"Xalta," the woman said.

Ariana didn't say anything further in case anyone was listening in. Xalta took her up four flights of stairs and then down a long hallway until they reached the end of it. "This is the largest room and has a view of the ocean on two sides."

"The ocean?" Ohmigoddess, where was she? Not in Kingwood Forest any longer, not if she could see the ocean.

"Aye. The duke loves to live on the ocean, but he can't cross the water in a boat."

"We are on an island?" Even worse, Ariana thought as she walked into the opulent bedchamber complete with a sitting area and a separate room connected to that was a private privy. The castle wasn't surrounded by a water-filled moat but an ocean! Tully's wizard was worth more than his weight in gold. She'd never heard of a wizard who could hide a whole island.

"Uh, aye." Xalta looked like maybe she shouldn't have mentioned it.

Ariana looked out the one window, and then the other. All she could see was ocean in both directions. No main continent at all. "Okay, so no problem. I would have guessed it as soon as I saw the ocean out of two of the windows." But where were they? "If Duke Tully doesn't use a boat to get to the mainland, how does he travel there?"

"By portal. Faraday made him a portal that he uses to return to the mainland with whomever he wishes to take." The maid opened a wardrobe and pulled out a long nightgown for Ariana to wear. The gown was white, and the sleeves were beautifully embroidered in white thread and so was the neckline and the hemline.

Ariana felt she would never get out of wearing all white clothing as a newbie angel. What was up with that anyway? She was working, or had been working advance assignments, well, one, but shouldn't she have been allowed to wear the colors she preferred now? White was so…white.

"Thanks." When the maid didn't leave, Ariana realized she was waiting to further assist her. "I can manage, thank you." Ariana wasn't royalty and she wasn't about to pretend she was, even if the duke wished to treat her as a duchess.

"Just pull that tassel on the wall and I'll know to come to assist you."

"Thanks. Uhm, are there any boats on the island?"

Xalta's eyes widened, then she smiled a little. "No boats. The only way we can leave the island is if Duke Tully takes us with him. He doesn't like the idea that anyone else could leave in a boat who doesn't get seasick. I'll leave you to get some sleep then."

Xalta left the chamber and shut the door and Ariana felt relieved she wasn't under anyone's scrutiny for the moment. She looked out one of the windows again. She was four flights up and the windows looked out on the cliffs high above a sandy beach below. No sign of any boats. What if her angel wings were really there, but just invisible to her because of the magic hiding the castle? If she climbed out of the window and her wings didn't appear when she jumped, would she still not be harmed because she was an angel after all? Since she didn't need to escape the chamber, just the castle, there was no sense in jumping out yonder window to test her theory.

Instead, she removed her boots and then she climbed onto the bed and jumped off it and tried to use her wings, but she landed hard on her feet with a thud, no wings appearing to help her out. What good was being an angel if a pesky dark magic wizard could turn her into an ordinary aura-less fae who couldn't even transport anywhere?

CHAPTER 10

*M*alik didn't want Halloran and the other dragons, including Ena, to accompany him to Kingwood Forest and the location of the magically hidden castle because he thought with only him and Brett involved, they might be able to slip in unnoticed. But Brett wouldn't do it on his own. They'd have to deal with not only a powerful wizard should they expose the castle, but also Duke Tully could send his soldiers out to engage them and a battle would ensue if Malik and Brett hadn't been able to sneak in and free Ariana.

Of course, Halloran still had it in mind to take Duke Tully hostage. If the duke had taken Ariana hostage, Malik was inclined to agree with the dragon this time.

It took hours for them to search through the forest, Brett casting magic every few minutes, getting nothing, though it was fascinating to see him work his magic. They finally made a camp and sat down to eat a lunch of boar stew. Working with dragons was a real boon. One of them shifted into his dragon scales and set the gathered wood for a campsite on fire, warming the food some of the men had brought with them.

"Exactly how does this magic detecting work?" Malik asked.

"It's like using a metal detector in the earth world. I can send tendrils out that seek out vibrations that will tell me if any magical artifacts are in the area. Some of us can sense magic in anything, like wizard-enforced magical artifacts. Or even if a person has inherent magical abilities. The castle is so large, you would think it would be easy to 'see.' But if the wizard is good enough, he can cast a spell of unseeing, where even the magic is hidden. I believe that's what he has done," Brett said.

"So we might not find it. Ever." Malik felt disheartened, but he would never give up looking for Ariana or searching for a way to break through the magical barrier to reach her. He would solicit the mage, Eleron, at the hawk fae castle next to assist him in locating and freeing Ariana if Brett had no luck.

Suddenly, Elwin and Juno arrived in the camp, both invisible to the dragon fae. Malik had a sinking feeling that Catriona had sent them to tell him to return home and explain to her just what had happened to Ariana.

"Catriona knows everything." For the first time, Elwin didn't sound like he was glad for it.

Juno nodded.

"She wants me to return, doesn't she?" Since Malik appeared to be talking to himself out loud, all conversation around the campfire abated and all eyes were upon him.

"Nope," Juno said. "She said her boss is upset with her for sending a newbie on this mission."

Malik closed his gaping mouth. "That can't be good."

"For you and Ariana it's good, because Catriona isn't going to turn you both into a puff of mist. As to this business of a magic user taking a guardian angel hostage, Catriona's boss is furious. Of course so is Catriona."

"So what are they going to do about it?" Malik figured the big angel guns were coming into play now and they'd sort it out.

"They sent us." Juno smiled.

Juno wasn't even working on advanced cases yet! Elwin and

Malik were, but Malik had to solicit a magic user to help so he didn't see that either Juno or Elwin's presence was going to make any difference. Though he had to admit he appreciated they'd come, even if it was because they were ordered to.

"Once we find the castle and can free Ariana, what exactly does Catriona want us to do? I mean with Tully?" Malik asked.

"Oh, he's on his own. He made his bed," Elwin said. "He might have been on the 'to save list,' but once he took an angel hostage, all bets are off."

Malik let out his breath. "All right. Why don't you reveal yourself to the dragon fae? We're all in this together." Then they did and Malik introduced them all to each other.

They ate with everyone else and then they were back to searching for the castle, but Brett wasn't getting anything.

Suddenly, Malik felt a warmth fill him from head to toe. He stopped in his footsteps. Ena and Juno were nearer to him and turned to look at him. "What?" they both asked.

And then he heard her whispered sigh. *Ariana's.* She was so close, he swore he could touch her.

"Ariana," he whispered, hoping she could hear him, but he was sure she couldn't. That it had just been his imagination and that he hadn't truly heard anything at all. "Where are you? I'm here. I've come for you. And so have Juno and Elwin." He figured, if she could hear him telling her that, she might be furious that Elwin was here after all he'd done to her. Yet if Elwin could assist in finding her and freeing her, that would help to make it up to her. "And the dragon fae mage, Brett."

Juno poked him in the shoulder. "What?"

"I swear I heard Ariana," Malik said.

"Saying what?" Juno asked.

What could he say to that? A whispered sigh?

"Ooh, just a whispery, mystery sound," Elwin said, making a good guess.

Malik knew Catriona shouldn't have sent Elwin to help with the case.

Brett had been listening in on the conversation. Well, several others were too. Brett began to cast his magic around near Malik and Elwin folded his arms, his face filled with skepticism.

"Here," Brett said. "Yet…then it's not." Brett motioned right next to Malik.

Did Malik have some connection with her somehow? Or maybe it had to do with Juno and Elwin being there too; that somehow, the three of them had helped to make a connection with her as angels united and it had penetrated the magic that was hiding her for just a split second.

"It's like she's there and I sensed a hint of magic, as if they went here and then left," Brett said.

Then a dark fae joined them. "This is Georgette," Ena said. "She's a dark fae tracker."

Some of the dark fae were known to be the best trackers of all the fae.

"Duke Tully has been here. He stood here." Georgette pointed to the same area Malik had sensed Ariana. "But then his fae dust trail is gone. It was here, and then vanished. He hadn't walked very far to arrive here either. He wasn't transported. I would be able to find where he was transported from."

"Angel transport then," Malik said. "Ariana brought him here, and he ensnared her in his magical trap."

"He's not a magic user," Brett said, "which means Duke Tully has hired a wizard to hide his castle, and in doing so, somehow, it's keeping Ariana there also."

"I guess as angels we don't have anything in our repertoire to counter the magic." Malik was angry about it. He had to get Ariana out of the duke's grasp and then? He was ready to turn the duke over to Halloran for his disposition, let Tully see how it felt to be placed in a dungeon without any way out.

"You sensed her before," Brett said.

"Yeah. It wasn't like she was talking to me or anything. I just felt her presence."

"Okay, well the problem is there may be a portal gateway in this vicinity, but there's no way for us to operate it or to actually locate it. Only the wizard who has created it, and Duke Tully, of course, can access it." Which was what Brett had said before, but Malik suspected he mentioned it for Juno and Elwin's benefit.

Malik rubbed his chin deep in thought. He couldn't believe they could be this close to her, possibly, and couldn't do anything about it.

"So what do we do?" Juno asked. "Nothing?"

"I'm staying here," Malik said. "I felt the connection to her here. Maybe I can reach out to her again."

Elwin sighed. "Okay, well, we have to stay here also. They said you have the lead on this, and we have to do everything you say, unless of course we have a better idea to get results."

"At least she's safe," Juno said. "Maybe not free, but I'm sure since she saved Tully's life, he wouldn't do anything to harm her."

"We'll stay too," Halloran said. "If we get a breakthrough, you'll need our help."

"Yeah," Ena said. "I agree."

Brett agreed too, which was good because he was the only magic user among them that could potentially be useful in their quest to locate Ariana, Malik believed.

* * *

ARIANA FELT SOMEONE TOUCH HER—HER mind, she thought, not her physical being. It was the most bizarre thing. Malik? Yes, it had been Malik. But she knew it wasn't possible. Then she was just waking when she heard someone enter her room.

Xalta. "Hello, the duke wished me to wake you in the event you were still asleep because he was afraid you wouldn't be able to sleep tonight otherwise."

So kind of him to care.

"Your wardrobe is filled with clothes. Choose anything you wish to wear, and if you'd like, I can show you all of the castle and its grounds," Xalta said.

"And the portal room?" Other than boats that Ariana could use to escape the island, that's the only other thing she really wanted to see. She had no plan to stay here any longer than she had to.

Xalta smiled as if she thought Ariana had a great sense of humor, but she was serious.

"Sure. I can show it to you. There's no sense in you searching for it on your own. You can't operate it, so the duke won't mind if you see it."

Great. Still, what if Ariana was able to somehow figure it out? She hurried to dress in a blue gown and brown suede boots. Finally, she was able to wear something other than white! "Does Faraday live here?" She assumed that if she could learn a way to operate the portal, Faraday would stop her. So she really was hoping he didn't live here.

"Oh, heaven's no. He has his own castle somewhere. No one knows where. We were surprised to see him arrive at the nooning meal. We suspect it was because the duke and his men had vanished, and then here you both show up. Then he came to see what had happened."

"Maybe he has the same kind of protection spell over his castle too."

"That could be. He's very secretive, like most wizards are. But he's even more so because he hides the duke's residence and the duke's an outlaw. That makes Faraday one too."

"Do you ever leave the castle and return to the mainland?" Ariana hoped Xalta could tell her more about where she'd end up once she was back on the mainland.

"No. I've been here since I was a girl. I haven't known any other place."

"Your family?"

"All gone."

"If I can find a way to leave the castle, would you want me to take you with me? I'd make sure you had a castle to reside in, if you liked. Or a village. You would be able to see the whole wide world, and not just this island."

Xalta didn't say anything for several moments, just straightening the room, that was already perfectly neat. Well, maybe the bed was a bit mussed up.

Maybe Ariana shouldn't have offered, but she felt if the woman needed saving, even if she wasn't on anyone's master guardian angel list, Ariana would do it.

"Ferdinand was with the men taken by the dragon fae." Xalta's eyes filled with tears. "Duke Tully abandoned them and even if they could have escaped the dragons, they wouldn't be able to return to the duke's castle unless he wished it."

"Ferdinand is someone important to you." Ariana didn't need affirmation. She knew it from seeing the woman's downcast expression.

Xalta brushed away tears.

"Okay, I promise if I can get out of here, and if I can take you with me, I'll do everything in my power to get Ferdinand released if the dragon fae have imprisoned him. The two of you, if that's what you both want, can stay with a household and start your lives over."

Xalta nodded.

"So all we need to do is find a way to leave here."

"There's a boat. The duke would have it destroyed if he knew about it. But some of the braver souls living here would sneak off when he was away kidnapping royals. Faraday would return to his castle. He doesn't bother coming here unless the duke summons him, or like in this case, the wizard got word that the dragons had captured some of his men and the duke had vanished."

"We can leave that way by boat?" So there truly was a boat!

"Only if the duke is gone. I can imagine him summoning the wizard and then he would sink the boat with all those who were aboard."

"Show me the portal device and the castle and grounds, as if we aren't doing anything more than that."

"All right." Then Xalta took her on a tour of the portal room first.

Inside the large room, the marble floors were well-polished, and a wall with a strange, blue light appearing on it made Ariana think that was where the portal was. "Have you ever seen the duke and others leave through here?"

"Aye, I had to bring rations and set them on the floor there. And then the duke put his hand on the wall over there and the portal opened, and they were able to go through it."

"Right here?" Ariana could see a handprint on the wall there where someone had placed their hand.

"Aye."

Ariana put her hand on the same place on the wall, but nothing happened. Not that she really thought anything would. But she had to try. To her amusement, Xalta put her hand on the same place, but there wasn't any change.

"I'll show you around the castle and then we'll go to the court-yard, the woods surrounding the castle, the cliffs, and the beach-es," Xalta said.

Ariana wanted to say something about the boat, but she was careful not to mention it as they began walking through the halls of the castle. She admired the tapestries on the walls, featuring pirates on the stormy sea—which she thought was ironic since Tully got seasick. He probably was able to afford the tapestries from all the ransoms he had been paid.

Xalta showed her the library and they went inside to look at the extensive number of books there. "There probably isn't anything we can learn from the books—I mean, as far as how to use the portal."

"What about a map of the island in relation to the mainland?" Ariana was desperate to see where she was in relation to the rest of the world. It was like when she first woke up in the angel realm and she had felt so disoriented.

Xalta's mouth dropped open. Then she hurried to a shelf and pulled out a book. "In here."

Ariana smiled. She'd never maneuvered a boat on the open ocean. She didn't have a clue as to where she was in relation to any place else, but if she could find a map to aid her, she might be able to pull it off.

Xalta set the large book on a table, and they began looking through the pages. "Here," Xalta said. "This is the duke's island. And this is the mainland."

Ariana was looking at the distance according to the map key and it appeared they had about twenty nautical miles to cover from the island to the mainland. Depending on the choppiness of the water, weather conditions, and how fast the boat could go, it could take them about two hours. The island was south of the dark fae kingdom. She realized she was a long way from home. Not the angel realm, but the hawk fae kingdom.

"Okay, this looks good." As long as they could leave in the boat without detection.

"The boat has a sail and oars. We should take a couple of men with us," Xalta said, "when we can go."

Ariana hoped it was soon because she was certain no one was coming to rescue her, even if they could. "*If* they don't tell on us. I hope the duke is leaving us soon."

Xalta shook her head. "They won't breathe a word. And Duke Tully is leaving soon. He's upset that he didn't get a hefty ransom from King Tiernan for Princess Esmeralda. He doesn't like to lose. It rarely happens. We figured he might be worried that people are on the lookout for him, but he also feels he lives a charmed life."

"Ha! He had a guardian angel protecting him. When is he leaving then?"

"He doesn't tell us his plans. Suddenly, we're scrambling to get food prepared and he's picking the people who will go with him. We have to be ready at a moment's notice. But from everything he's said, he's going back out there as soon as possible."

"At night, right?" That could be a problem for sailing at night, but she figured Duke Tully would want to leave at that time so he could be set up to grab the unsuspecting hostage as soon as one passed by.

"Always. That's why we need a couple of the men to go with us because they've done this at night when the duke's been gone. He's usually away for several days."

"Do you know anyone who would agree to take us with them?"

"Because you're a guardian angel and they know how much that will upset him if they free you?" Xalta asked.

"Right, but who knows? I might be able to save one of them at some future time. Here, I can't do anything for anyone."

"I'm sure they'd be more worried about what he and his wizard would do to them."

"I guess there is no hiding who I am."

"Not at all. Everyone in the whole court knows who and exactly what you are."

They headed outside the castle walls and Ariana kept thinking she'd see Kingwood Forest, just like she'd left it when she'd entered the castle, but instead she saw windswept waves slamming into the sandy beach down below. They walked down to the beach, and she noticed rare seashells shimmering all along it. How beautiful. And then they headed to the cliffs that stretched up to where her room was.

"Where's the boat?" Ariana asked. No one was out here. Everyone was inside working, doing their chores.

"I can't show it to you. If the duke were to learn of it, he'd destroy it and who knows what he would do to anyone who had built it or used it to reach the mainland. When it's time to go, we'll just go."

"All right." Ariana wished she could at least see the boat so she had a clue about what she was getting herself into. Then she went with Xalta back to the castle and she couldn't believe it was already time for dinner. She was trying not to show her nervousness while sitting beside the duke, when she had plans to escape by boat as soon as she could.

"Did you enjoy the walk through the castle and grounds?" Tully asked.

"Yes. You have a beautiful castle." Adorned with all kinds of treasures that he hadn't come by honestly, she suspected.

"And what did you think of the portal room?"

"It was…austere." There were no ornaments, tapestries, nothing in the barren room.

"Nothing to take away from the usefulness of the room that has only one purpose. Did you see my extensive library?" he asked.

"I did."

"You can borrow any book to read at any time."

And a boat? A map of the area was the only thing Ariana had been interested in reading in his library. She wanted to ask him when he was leaving the castle!

"Thanks. I appreciate it."

They were eating halibut, her favorite seafood. If she hadn't learned that his island was closer to the dark fae region down south, she might have believed the fish came from the ocean near where the hawk fae and island griffin fae were located. She would think, before the wizard had hidden Tully's island, someone would have known it existed.

"So what is the name of your island?"

"Mystic Island. Appropriate, isn't it?"

"I guess so. Who named it as such?" Tully? Or someone before him?

"The ancient fae. It was uninhabited until my ancestors took control of it and have ruled it for an eternity."

"It must have been visible at some point."

"Faraday's ancestors were the first who made the island invisible, once we built on it. That way we never have any trouble with other kingdoms warring with us like the island griffin fae with the mainland fae kinds."

"But then you started taking hostages. No one else in your family, right?"

"Aye. It might be nice to have a peaceful existence here, no strife with any other kind, but it's well, boring, to say the least."

Boring. So for thrills, and gain, he took hostages.

After the meal, the duke asked her, "Do you need anything further tonight?"

Just for you to use the portal room and me to take a boat out of here. "No, thank you. I'll be fine."

"Okay, good. Xalta will be sleeping on a trundle bed in your chamber so she'll be at your beck and call."

Just like if Ariana had been royalty. She wanted to say it wasn't necessary, but she figured this was the best situation of all. They would be together and if they learned the duke was leaving, they would be able to move more quickly.

But had Xalta been able to find a crew for the boat who would agree to take them with them? She sure hoped so. She had another idea though, if the men didn't agree to it. They could take word to someone, who could tell the dragon fae that she was Duke Tully's hostage. Though the problem with that was the men might not want to let anyone know where she was, or the duke could want their heads if he was to learn of it.

Once she returned to the chamber, she paced, hoping that

Xalta would be there soon so they could discuss the situation. She didn't have to wait too long before Xalta arrived.

Xalta hurried into the room, closed the door, and whispered, "Five men are helping."

Ariana was surprised and thrilled.

"They said they're keeping a watch out on the duke and as soon as they know he's gone, one of them will come for us and we'll head down to the beach."

"Okay, good."

"But if Tully does go tonight, we have a problem."

"What is wrong?"

"The seas are rough. Normally, they don't try to navigate during a stormy night, but they're more worried about keeping you here."

"Why?" Did they think Ariana could hurt them in some way? Or maybe that her angel bosses might?

"They're afraid if they need a guardian angel, they won't get one because the angels above will know they're helping to keep you here. So they want to take you away from here with haste. They want you to put in a good word with the angels."

Ariana smiled. She would do that, once she got herself out of trouble with Catriona.

She crossed the floor to the window and looked out at the setting sun. The whitecaps were whipping up on the crest of the waves, and she had an uneasy feeling. What if the boat capsized and she had to save these people who were trying to get her safely to the mainland in dangerous waters? If she could get beyond the magical spell surrounding the island and her ability to transport—well, then everyone else would be able to also. So that would be a good thing.

"Can people transport from the boat once they've moved beyond the island and its magical spell?"

"No," Xalta said, getting her trundle bed ready so she could lie down. "The ocean floor is filled with iron ore, so no one can transport themselves over the water."

Which made sense because that's the way it was between the hawk fae and the island of the griffin fae. That's why Princess Esmeralda hadn't been able to escape except by boat.

But Ariana noticed that Xalta wasn't getting changed into nightclothes. Instead, she was packing a small bag and setting it next to her bed.

"Do you want me to wrap up some of your things too?" Xalta asked.

"If this works, I'll be returning to the angel realm and won't need these clothes."

"But you might need some until that happens."

"All right." And for the boat passage too. Ariana pulled out breeches and a tunic to wear on the boat.

"Here's a waterproof jacket and pants to go over the other clothes you're wearing. We won't put them on until we reach the boat or anyone who sees us will wonder what's going on. You'll have to wear it on the boat, otherwise you'll be soaked on the trip."

Ariana changed clothes, hoping that the duke didn't come to see her dressed liked that and wonder why she wasn't dressed for bed. She bundled up a few items that she could wear once they were on the shore of the mainland until she could make sure her angel wings were working and then she and Xalta would go to the dragon fae kingdom and find a way to have Ferdinand released. She just hoped when she made it out of the duke's reaches, she could actually convince the dragon fae to take care of Ferdinand and Xalta. For sure, they would give Xalta a job for arranging for Ariana's freedom. Ferdinand had been there with the duke when he held Princess Esmeralda hostage, so that was another story.

CHAPTER 11

"*I*f I'm correct in my assumption that the duke has a way to travel to different regions to set up a trap for other unsuspecting wealthy fae, he won't have to return here. Not when he might believe we'll be looking for him for having taken Princess Esmeralda hostage." Brett poked a stick at the campfire still burning.

"So where do we go? Can you give an educated guess as to where he might end up next?" Malik was exasperated. He wanted to do something. *Anything.*

"Can you feel any connection to her still?" Juno asked.

Malik shook his head. "How does the duke even know when wealthy travelers will be on some of these roads? I could envision him sitting on a particular road for days waiting for a wealthy traveler to pass by. Someone could see him and his men and report them."

"It's possible his wizard has an eye on the fae world and can advise him where to go. The other notion is that the duke has spies at all the major kingdoms, which is possible," Brett said, "but I think that more unlikely."

"You will have to eliminate the wizard," Elwin said.

"That would help to put an end to the duke's hostage-taking ways," Malik said.

"That's easier said than done. I have no idea what kinds of magic the duke's wizard can wield. If he can aid the duke in finding victims, and keep his castle hidden always, he must be very powerful. I don't know his name or where he's from so I haven't a clue about him," Brett said.

Malik knew he was supposed to be here to save lives, not put them at risk, but he sure wouldn't mind helping Brett to eliminate the wizard.

"None of us will do any good without some sleep," Ena said. "Except for a couple of dragons who will serve on guard duty at all times, the rest of us will need to sleep. At least the weather is pleasant enough out tonight."

Malik looked up at the star-filled night and wondered if Ariana could see them too. *Where are you, Ariana?*

* * *

ARIANA WAS sound asleep when she heard movement in the bedchamber and saw a man holding a lantern. She quickly sat up in bed.

"Are you ready, Xalta?" a black-haired and bearded man asked, his voice hushed.

"Aye, we both are." Xalta threw her covers aside and lit a lantern.

Ariana hurried to climb out of bed, slipped on her boots, and grabbed her bag of clothes.

"The duke left a half hour ago. We've been readying the boat in the meantime and didn't want the two of you down there in the event anyone was curious as to what we were doing on such a stormy night. If Xalta didn't tell you, we often take a few of us to shore when the duke is gone, or we'd go stir crazy on the island. Some don't mind never leaving it. But others of us can't deal with it as well. So no one tells on any of us when we make these excursions. Taking you along with us could make a difference," he said to Ariana. "I hate to say the weather is very bad for an ocean crossing and we normally wouldn't take the chance to sail, but we cannot delay the journey. Rumors abound that Faraday plans to ferret you away at his first opportunity and we won't have another chance to free you." He led them out of the chamber, and they were quiet as they hurried through the corridors, careful not to make a sound.

Ariana had worried that Faraday wasn't giving her up that easily. He had all the power, for one thing. As they headed down yet another hall, she didn't think anyone would have heard them anyway for the loud sound of thunder booming overhead, and the wild display of lightning brightening up the sky intermittently. Rain was pouring down and she wondered how she could have slept through any of it.

Before they left the castle and went down to the beach, they donned their waterproof jackets and pants and pulled up their hoods. Then the man led them out through the castle gates and down to the beach. To her surprise, nine other men were waiting for them. She had considered trying to save one or two of the people if she had to with flying as an angel wing, if she even had them, but that many? She was afraid she would never manage.

"They all heard what we were doing and wanted to help," the man explained to her.

She suspected they all wanted to get in her good graces in case they needed her sometime in their lives. She didn't dare tell them she had no idea who she was supposed to save until the time came. One thing she realized—her saving Tully from the dragons—should have taught him a lesson. But it hadn't. She suspected that meant she hadn't gotten credit for this mission either, despite it being sanctioned.

Would Catriona put Ariana back on simple missions until she could get it right then?

Then the men hurried to load both Ariana and Xalta into the boat. Some of them joined the women, and the rest shoved the boat into the water and climbed aboard. It was time to break away from the magic surrounding the island, but first the men had to row against the breaker waves and strong currents. It was a good thing they had brought more men, or they wouldn't have made it, she didn't think.

"Can I help?" Ariana asked, wanting to do anything to assist them in aiding her to escape the island.

"If you could quiet the ocean, we would be grateful, but we're certain you cannot, so stay as dry and warm as you can belowdecks. We would not want to lose you when a wave breaks over the decks," the man who had come for them said.

"Tie me to the ship." Ariana wasn't going to go below deck. If the ship began to sink, she would be there to help save someone, hopefully more people. She couldn't do that from a cabin hidden in the bowels of the boat.

What they truly needed though was magic strong enough to protect them from the storm as the rain pummeled them and the winds were so strong, the sailors were rowing like madmen and at the same time, fighting being torn from their posts.

The bearded man tied her to the ship and Xalta wanted to stay with her, so he roped her in near Ariana, so the two women could huddle together. The waves rose all around them, some crashing over the deck.

She and Xalta were terrified, and she imagined the men were too. She didn't think they'd make it in this storm.

"Where are we headed now?" she asked, because from what she could see, which was very little, they were headed away from where she thought the mainland was.

"We have to go way around the shoals to avoid crashing the boat on the rocks," one of the men said. "Then we'll head back toward the mainland."

"Great." Lightning struck the water off in the distance, and she cringed. The waves smashed into the boat with a vengeance, the water slamming onto the deck, threatening to wash everyone away and would have if they hadn't been strapped down. But she worried about the boat flipping over and then everyone would be tied to the boat and unable to free themselves, unlike with the earlier rescue she had done where she had saved the man with the overturned canoe in the Gulf during the storm.

Except for the flashes of lightning continually illuminating the sky, everything appeared inky black: the sky, the sea, and the rain that was pouring down in a deluge. The rain was hitting everyone so hard, she had a hard time making out where they were going. She wondered how they could see to row in the right direction.

She thought of trying to feel if her wings were there now so she could spread them, but she was wearing the waterproof jacket and she couldn't tell if they were under her jacket. They would be folded against her back, and she might not be able to feel them because of the waves slamming into her. Was the magic over the island extending some distance out and was still affecting the appearance of her wings?

But then she wondered if it was as she had earlier suspected, that Catriona had removed her wings because Ariana had taken the duke to the angel realm. She needed them if she had to rescue the crew.

Then what she was worried about occurring—happened. A rogue wave of giant proportions slammed into the boat. The boat was rolling over...over...over and it was upside down. With shrieks and screams and yells, everyone was trying to untie the ropes securing them to the boat. Everyone's worst nightmare had just been realized as they ended up in the broiling sea, grabbing for ropes tied to the boat still or anything that would keep them afloat.

Everyone was attempting to cling onto the boat but Ariana. She was trying to pull off her waterproof pants and jacket so she could try to see if she had her wings so she could help those in the sea now. She shouted, "Is everyone accounted for?"

They were all carried up with the boat on another swell of a wave and then slammed into another trough. She finally kicked off her boots, and yanked off the waterproof pants she was wearing, both weighing her down.

"Xalta!" one of the men shouted.

Ariana realized she didn't see her either. Xalta didn't answer when he called her name.

Praying she was safe under the boat and on the chance she might not have freed herself from the rope tying her to it, Ariana dove under the water and the vessel, looking for her. "Xalta!" she called out in the pitch blackness as soon as she surfaced below the overturned boat.

"Here," Xalta said, sounding as waterlogged as Ariana felt. She wasn't too far away, and Ariana swam over to her.

"Can you swim?"

"Aye, we all know how to since we live on an island. I hadn't been able to untie my rope when the boat capsized. I just managed to finish untying it now."

"Okay, good. Come with me then."

Xalta and Ariana swam out from underneath the boat and joined the men.

"Is everyone else here?" Ariana asked, while all hands tried to keep their heads above water. She could see a few gashes on peoples' faces where they had been injured. She hoped no one would bleed into the water and attract sharks.

"Aye, everyone," one of the men said.

"All right. This boat is probably too heavy to flip over." Ariana explained how she had helped a paddler flip his canoe in a storm.

"It's too heavy," one of the men said, confirming her suspicion.

"Will the currents carry us to the mainland?" she asked, hopeful that it would, but afraid they'd be swept back to the island.

"No. It will carry us out to sea."

Okay, so that wasn't good either.

"Which way do we need to go to reach the mainland?" she asked, trying to come up with a plan.

"Off that way. To the west." A man motioned behind her.

"Do you have any idea how far that is?" She was still trying to peel off her jacket, while holding onto the boat with one hand. She finally managed to lose the jacket.

"Maybe fifteen miles."

"Okay." She sure wished they could all transport themselves to the mainland. She tried to make her wings appear. She wasn't sure if they were behind her the way the waves were pummeling her, but then she thought they might be, and she tried to spread them. Against the water, it was nearly impossible. Would she break them? Would they be too wet to fly with? She felt the pressure on her back and then she realized she was actually feeling her wings. That was good news, but then she worried, what if they were waterlogged? She'd heard conflicting stories about that.

But she had to try it—to fly out of the water, above the waves, though she was worried about the lightning strikes. She lifted out of the water and into the pouring rain, her powerful wings flapping—just like they were duck's wings, impervious to the rain.

Yes! At least something had worked.

Everyone was looking at her in shock, and then she swooped down and grabbed Xalta up out of the water, hugging her close to her. "If I can make it to the mainland with Xalta, I will return for each of you." She wasn't sure she could make it that far with that many people, but she was a guardian angel, and *this* was her mission now.

"Goddess speed," several of the men said.

And she prayed she would make it back for all of them and wouldn't lose them in the sea, or that she would even find her way to the mainland at all. Well, back to the boat again also. Nothing was guaranteed.

"I'll be back," she promised. Then she flew with all her might through the storm and hurried to find the mainland. She had flown for what seemed like forever when she saw lights off in the distance. And that had to be from a building on land or a boat's lights.

Xalta had been quiet until then, maybe afraid of being carried through the storm with the lightning striking all over the place like this and even more concerned they wouldn't find their way to the mainland. "Lights. A lighthouse!"

"I see it. I'm going to drop you off by the lighthouse. Get word to the keeper we need help. I'm going back to the boat for one of the men." And then Ariana set Xalta on the land and the maid ran, screaming at the top of her lungs for help.

"We need help! Anyone, please! We need help!" Xalta cried out.

Good, Xalta was taking action and not too traumatized. Then Ariana was up in the air again, flying her hardest, trying to beat the wind and she realized it was a headwind this time, whereas she'd had a tailwind going to the mainland. She wasn't sure how far it really had been, but she kept going on the same path as she had taken before. She could see her dust trail, which confused her. It wasn't an angel's dust trail. They didn't leave one. It was her hawk fae dust trail, but she didn't have it any longer. Not once since she'd become an angel. What was that all about? But it helped her to find her way back to the men and she was sure she couldn't have made it otherwise. Thank the goddess!

She finally saw the boat up on top of a wave and the men still clinging to it. She swooped down and reached for a man, pulling him out of the water, and the others cheered.

So many men, and she was afraid it would take too long for her to get all of them. But she kept going, kept flying. She wouldn't quit until she'd rescued as many as she could.

When she reached the shore with the first of the men, a group of dark fae were gathered, trying to launch a boat. But the seas were so rough still, she couldn't rely on them to rescue the men in time.

"An angel," one of the dark fae said.

"She is, and she has saved our lives," the man said as she set him down on the ground.

Then she flew off and was headed back to the capsized boat. She managed to rescue three more men, taking each to the mainland one after another. She was feeling weary, but the dark faes' boat was having just as much of a struggle to row through the waves as Tully's boat had before it capsized.

When she reached Tully's men clinging to the overturned boat, she was afraid there were fewer left. Fewer than there should have been.

"They've taken refuge against the rain under the boat," one of the men said.

"Okay, well, you, come with me then."

Then she dove for him and carried him off. "A boat is coming for you. The dark fae are trying to reach your boat, but they're having as much trouble in the storm as you had." She was hoping they wouldn't capsize next, and she'd have to rescue them too! She had way too many people still to save as it was.

Then she saw the dark fae boat and it was heading back in. No! But she didn't really blame them either. It could be a disaster, and these were Tully's men, responsible for helping him take people hostage so the dark fae might not see them in a good light.

But the dark fae sailors waved at her, and she dropped onto the boat, and they took care of Tully's man. Then she flew off again. At least she didn't have to fly back as far this time. But when she returned to Tully's men's boat, all the men who were left were waiting for her, none of them under the boat, none of them wanting to be left behind.

They looked worried, probably because she had returned so

quickly. "The dark fae couldn't make it in their boat in the storm. I dropped off your man on their boat though. I'll take another one to their boat as they return to the mainland. It won't be as long a journey." She dove down to get another man and then she managed to reach the dark fae boat again before they had gotten too far. Then she flew back for another man. That's when she saw three angels headed her way—Malik! And Juno and Elwin. Each of them descended to grab one last man and she guided them to the dark fae boat. Right before they got there, a rogue wave hit their boat and her heart nearly gave out as she watched in horror as the boat was tossed about like a toy boat in the sea. The dark fae boat capsized, and now the men she'd set upon it and the dark fae were all in the water.

"Come on," Malik said. "We'll take these men to shore and come back for the rest."

"That's easy for you to say. This is your first rescue." She was about worn out, but she wasn't giving up now. Not when she knew they could all do it together.

He gave her a small smile.

Goddess, she was glad to see him. She could give him a hug. "I thought we both might have lost our wings."

"Not us. They were needed tonight more than any other night I've served the angel realm," Malik said.

"What are you both doing here?" Ariana asked Juno and Elwin.

"Assisting you," Juno said.

"Saving you," Elwin said.

Ariana scoffed. "I had to save myself. You're helping to save others who tried to free me from Tully's imprisonment."

Then they landed on the mainland, leaving the four men there and headed back out to pick up those who had been on the dark fae's capsized boat. She hoped they weren't too angered they'd lost their own boat while trying to rescue Tully's men.

"If you need a break, after this, take one," Malik said to her.

"We've seen all the men and women you've saved already. You have to be worn out."

She wasn't quitting until the last man and woman were on dry ground. Well, wet ground. The rains and winds hadn't let up, but thankfully, the lightning seemed to be moving north of them.

At least the dark fae boat was closer to the mainland so they didn't have to fly as far.

"How did you get here? The last place I was at was Kingwood Forest. How did you learn that I was in the dark fae territory?" Ariana asked, surprised to see them, but sure glad for it.

"A dark fae tracker was with us. Brett tried to figure out where you were, but he said the wizard's sorcery was too powerful."

"Faraday. That's the name of the wizard."

"We'll have to tell Brett, after we finish rescuing the sailors. He and the other dragon fae will be joining us soon."

"I don't understand how the dark fae tracker could locate me. I didn't leave a trail." At least Ariana hadn't before. She didn't think. Unless she just hadn't noticed it until now.

Malik glanced back at the trail she was leaving. "You are. It reappeared somehow. It doesn't make any sense. You're an angel, but your hawk fae aura is shimmering. That's not something that's supposed to happen."

"So why is it?" She was about to lose her angel wings...permanently? If so, let her at least finish this mission, *please*.

CHAPTER 12

*M*alik didn't want to speculate why Ariana's aura was visible or why she was leaving a fae dust trail now. At least he didn't want to say out loud what he was thinking. He didn't think it could be, but what if Ariana was turning into her fae self again? What if she was losing her angel status? He couldn't imagine anything like that happening, but what if? He'd lose her again. And here she'd finally said she would be his girlfriend.

Ariana was exhausted and he worried about her collapsing in the sea due to overexertion. She kept trying to keep up with him while she was flying back with him and the others to rescue the people still floundering in the high swells of water.

He slowed down for her, but she wouldn't fly any slower. Okay, so he was trying to keep her safe and he was going to do it, no matter what. Then they were at the boat again and the rain was slowing down, the waves still large swells though. The four of them took more men and a woman and headed back to the shore.

Wagons were transporting the people they'd dropped off already at the shore to the castle. He hoped they were caring for

Tully's men and not incarcerating them after they tried to get Ariana to safety.

"You didn't give up on me," Ariana said as they went back out again.

The waves were finally beginning to settle down and the dark fae were launching another boat.

"Are you kidding?" Malik shook his head. "I finally got you to agree to date me."

"Let's take a ride on the dark fae boat." Juno sounded like she was worn out, but Malik wondered if she only said so to try and get Ariana to agree to rest. "That way we can help fish the men out of the water once the boat reaches them."

Ariana was the one who truly needed to take it easy, but she wasn't quitting. She was right back out there, flying past the new dark fae boat, eager, but weary and Malik could see she was fumbling with more of the victims each time she picked up another of the sailors now.

He understood how she felt. The longer the men were in the water, the worse off they would be, and they needed to get them out of the water quickly. If it meant pulling them out of the sea where they could be experiencing hypothermia or facing shark attacks, and then dropping them off on the boat, that should work. Maybe they could even get the rest of them to the boat and then they wouldn't have to row out so far and once everyone was onboard the new vessel, they could take the sailors back to shore.

Which was just what they did. The angels carried the men in several more trips to the dark fae boat. Each time the angels returned to fish out some more men, the dark fae sailors in the water told them to take Tully's men first because they had been in the water longer after their own boat had capsized. That was remarkable, both because they were Tully's men and had at one time taken the dark fae queen's daughter, Princess Ritasia, hostage, though she was now queen of the hawk fae. And also because the dark fae, also known as the lion fae, were known to be fierce warriors and protective of their own kind first.

Malik wondered if the dark fae were on their best behavior because they hoped to be rewarded with a guardian angel's help some time in the future.

They might be. Who knew? For now, he was concentrating on Ariana to make sure she didn't give out while rescuing the last few sailors. Once everyone was onboard, the dark fae boat headed back into shore, and Malik and the other angels rode with them. Malik would have flown back, and he suspected Elwin would have too, but he wanted to make sure that Ariana rested her wings after the workout she'd had. He was certain if they flew to shore, she would have too.

When they saw the mainland, crowds of fae were waiting for them. He hoped this was good news, not bad. But as they got closer, the people cheered them. Or the dark fae sailors' return, maybe. Or possibly both.

What he hadn't expected was for them to take everyone inside the castle to clean up, provide clean, dry clothes, bandage wounds, and then have a big celebration once everyone had been taken care of.

Queen Irenis hugged Ariana and then they sat down at the head table to partake of the feast. "I can't thank you enough for saving Ritasia, and Tiernan, also, of course, but I'm so sorry to hear that you aren't...um, with us any longer."

Ariana smiled at her. "I am with you. Just in a different way."

"Why...I can't help but notice that your aura is faintly visible, that you leave a fae dust trail, but that the other angels don't. Is that because you are so newly turned?" the queen asked.

Malik was eating his Cornish hen but listening in on what the queen was saying to Ariana. He realized how important Ariana had been at her former job. He knew she was, but it was different hearing it from others.

But the issue with Ariana's fae dust trail and aura was totally off. And he wondered what was up with it. He knew he hadn't missed seeing it before. She hadn't had it once she became an angel.

He was sitting on the other side of Ariana and next to him, Juno was seated. He turned to her. "Do you see that Ariana's hawk fae aura has reappeared?" He hoped that Juno had seen the same thing as him, and that he hadn't just imagined she didn't have it before.

"Uh, yeah."

Elwin leaned forward on the other side of Juno. "You know what that means, don't you?"

"What?" Malik didn't want to reveal what he thought this all meant in case he was wrong.

"She's not going to be one of us for very much longer." Elwin sat back in his chair.

"No way," Juno said. "She's barely been with us for any time at all. I'd heard rumors some angel fae were given a chance to return to the fae world, but I've never known of anyone who has for real. And she just joined us!"

"She's special, Catriona said." Though Malik knew that Elwin was supposedly also. If being special meant she could sometime return to the fae world, why hadn't Elwin? Malik knew she wanted to return to the hawk fae kingdom to work as a royal guard. Would she even be able to get her job back? Most likely, after she had come to the king's sister's aid.

If all of this was the case, he was glad for her, but extremely disappointed for himself. He really wanted to get to know her better. To date her, whether Catriona sanctioned it or not. He wanted to be Ariana's good friend, but if she was a fae again, he wouldn't be able to see her like he wanted to. Certainly not like he could now.

"*I'm* special," Elwin said, sitting up taller. "But I don't have my aura returning. No fae dust trail."

"She's more special than you then, Elwin," Juno said, sounding haughty about it.

Malik smiled, but then he lost the smile. He didn't want to lose Ariana to the fae world.

Ariana had been speaking to the queen and he was impressed that they spoke to each other like they were the best of friends. He admired that about Ariana. The dark fae queen was known to be aloof to non-royals.

Then the queen spoke to her advisor on the other side of her, and Ariana turned to lean over and kiss Malik's cheek. But that wasn't enough for him, and he didn't care if anyone else saw, his angel cohorts, for one. He kissed her mouth and she kissed him back, eager to let him know she was so glad to be with him again. Still, he was worried about her losing her angel wings.

"So how bad is it going to be when we return to the angel realm?" Ariana sounded worried.

He hadn't had a chance to tell her that Catriona's boss was involved in this and could be upset with Catriona for assigning Ariana a case this difficult after she'd just started working for them. He told her about it now.

Ariana's jaw dropped. "Oh, no, that's not good. Another thing though. I promised Xalta, the woman who helped me escape Duke Tully's island, Mystic Island was what he called it, that I would help her free her friend, Ferdinand, from the dragon fae's castle, if he's incarcerated."

Malik sat back in his chair. "Okay."

"You don't think we'll be allowed to do it? I'm doing it. I promised." Ariana looked at him in a way that said she was doing this no matter what *he* wanted to do.

Sighing, he reached out and took her hand and squeezed it with reassurance. "I'm going with you. Now, Catriona may say something else about it. She might force me to return to the angel realm. But in the meantime, I'm going with you."

"Where are you going?" Juno asked.

"To the dragon fae kingdom," Malik said.

Juno patted Elwin on the shoulder. "Looks like our mission isn't finished here just yet."

Malik was glad Juno and Elwin, it appeared, were going with them. Though he hoped they wouldn't get into trouble for not returning to the angel realm right away now that they had Ariana in hand.

Since Brett, Ena, and Halloran and some of their other dragons had finally arrived, they would be returning with them. If Duke Tully showed up in their path, he'd be apprehended at once.

Before they finished their meal, Ariana suddenly glanced over at a man sitting at one of the lower tables and studied him so thoroughly, her whole body shifting from relaxed to tense, Malik knew she recognized the man and not in a good way.

He was going to ask her what was wrong, but she suddenly vanished and appeared next to the man, grabbing his arm, and shouting, "*He* is an assassin!"

Which could be true. They did have an assassin guild in the lion fae kingdom, but then Malik realized if Ariana knew that, he must have threatened the hawk fae royal family when she'd been protecting them.

Malik was instantly at her side to protect her. Guards had rushed forth to clamp the dark fae in irons before he could escape, if he had planned to. But he could have already, and he didn't seem to have anything to hide. Which made the situation seem curiouser than before.

The queen motioned for her guards to bring the man to the high table. When they joined her, Queen Irenis said to Ariana, "Rex is with the assassins' guild here in the lion fae territory. What is this man to you, Ariana?"

"He shot an arrow at King Tiernan while he was on a hunt, attempting to kill him. The assassin was using a crimson bow. I knocked him down and still have his crimson bow." If looks could kill, Ariana appeared to want to eliminate the dark fae on the spot, her hands clenched tightly and her face wearing a fearsome scowl.

Malik was thinking she didn't have the crimson bow with her. She had to have left it behind in the hawk fae kingdom before she had left for South Padre Island and died.

"And who paid for this assassination?" the queen asked Rex, looking imperious now on her throne at the high table.

Malik had heard she wasn't very forgiving.

"A hawk fae by the name of Claude. He wanted me to kill a royal guard and pretend to make an assassination attempt on the king. It was to look like I had made an attempt on the king's life, the guard had successfully protected the king, but had taken the arrow for him and died."

The queen arched a dark brow in question. "You never miss."

The dark fae cast her a small, knowing smile and inclined his head toward Ariana. "Ariana was to be my target."

Ariana's jaw dropped. Malik was so angry, he could kill Claude with his bare hands.

"I couldn't do it. She was just too...intriguing." Rex turned to Ariana. "You know, that was my favorite bow and if I'd wanted to steal *you* and my bow away, I could have. For your own protection, of course. But this Claude person was a coward to hire an assassin to kill you. And I assumed he had some beef with you. I figured you would be hailed a hero and he would have lost out."

"Are you satisfied with Rex's explanation?" Queen Irenis asked Ariana.

Ariana looked like she was having a difficult time letting go of the grudge. Then she cast Rex an evil smile. "Maybe you would like to finish your quest and instead of taking me down, you can deal with Claude."

Rex gave her just as dark a smile back. "And what would I get for my effort?"

"A crimson bow? I hear it could be your favorite."

Rex chuckled. "How about I return with you, since you are going to the hawk fae kingdom, are you not? And I can out the traitor? For one well-worn crimson bow. It was my father's and my grandfather's bow before that."

"We have a deal." Ariana shook his hand to seal the bargain. "Did you get paid in full to assassinate me?"

"Half. It was worth it to see who Claude desperately wanted to kill, though I sorely missed my bow. It was a fair trade though so that you could prove you had protected the king. So what was Claude's reason for wishing you dead?"

"He is my ex-boyfriend."

Rex shook his head. "He truly is a coward then."

"Is the situation resolved to your satisfaction?" the queen asked Ariana.

"It is," Ariana said, and then the queen ordered her guards to remove the dark fae's shackles and everyone returned to their seats to eat their meals.

"Do you believe him?" Malik asked Ariana. He wasn't about to take the dark fae's word for it. What if it had just been one of his off days? And he'd missed his true target—King Tiernan? What if he was just trying to save face because he hadn't made his target, and now his queen was questioning him about it, ready to terminate him if he didn't answer her correctly?

"Yes. I wondered why he hadn't killed me and taken his bow from me, or vanished, taking me and his bow with him. And it all makes sense. Claude was angry with me when I broke up with him because I'd caught him kissing another fae. Rex was hiding his dark fae aura, so I didn't know he could be with the assassin guild. The queen is right. They normally never miss their target. If I'm unable to return to the hawk fae kingdom because of angel duties, then he can take word to the king, along with the dragon fae here who have witnessed his testimony, and the king can deal with Claude."

"I'd like to deal with him," Malik said, still angry that any fae would attempt to have her murdered.

She smiled at him, her expression more lighthearted and then she reached over and patted his hand. "Believe me, the royal family will take care of him."

Malik sure hoped so because he planned to if they didn't.

They finished their meal, and the queen was putting everyone up for the night. And Malik realized the duke's men wouldn't be able to return to the duke's island. Their boat was gone. "What's going to happen to the duke's men now, Halloran?"

"The duke's men will be taken in by the dragon fae. They are dragon fae, just not shifters. They will be given jobs that have nothing to do with taking hostages. But for now, everyone needs to rest up until we leave in the morning."

Everyone thanked the queen for her generosity and the dark fae for their involvement in rescuing the duke's men.

Xalta wanted to stay with Ariana for the night, and Ariana seemed to be agreeable, the two of them appearing to be fast friends.

"I guess that means I have to fend for myself," Juno said.

"Of course not. You and Xalta will room with me. The guys can stay together. The queen has made special accommodations for all of us," Ariana said, appearing to be thrilled the ladies were all sharing a chamber.

Now *Elwin* looked impressed that the queen had made special arrangements for them—particularly since they figured it all had to do with Ariana.

CHAPTER 13

*A*riana settled down on a canopied bed and Xalta and Juno each had trundle beds next to hers. "Okay, so why is my aura showing? Malik won't tell me what he knows, like he's afraid to say. Am I going to dissolve into dust? Or turn into a puff of mist?"

"Well, we talked about it," Juno admitted, the ladies all wearing borrowed white shifts to sleep in because they didn't have any clothes of their own with them. The bags Ariana and Xalta had brought with them were probably at the bottom of the deep blue sea by now.

"And?"

Xalta's eyes were huge. She looked like she didn't know if she should even be here during this discussion because she wasn't an angel.

Juno let out her breath and gave an exaggerated sigh. "We don't know, for sure. But we think it might be that you're becom-ing…uh, well, a fae again."

Ariana had wondered, but she had thought she'd have to do something really illegal to do it. Then again, she guessed what she had done—saving the fae from the ship, not teaching Tully a lesson, getting herself taken hostage, even taking him to the angel realm, she'd been doing everything wrong.

"Do you know anyone who has returned to the fae world as a fae?" Ariana asked.

"Not personally, no. But of course there have been rumors. We don't know why it would be happening to you, except that Catriona had said earlier you were special."

"She said the same thing about Elwin," Ariana said.

"Aye, but maybe you're special in a different way. One that means you could return to your world, to your former life."

"Would you want that?" Xalta asked. "Your wings are so beautiful."

"Yes, I wanted to return to the fae world in the worst way. I wanted to be with my father and my friends and back on the staff with the hawk fae royal guard."

"What about Malik?" Xalta asked, sounding concerned.

Yeah, he was a problem. Ariana didn't want to leave him behind and she knew she wouldn't be able to see him if any of this was even possible. She wanted to be happy about returning to the fae world, but things had changed for her. How would her father feel if she suddenly was alive again? Would she even have a job on King Tiernan's staff any longer?

"Yeah, I would wish he could come with me," Ariana said.

"I figured that. We aren't supposed to get involved with other fae in the angel realm, as far as we know, though no one has stated so for sure, like it's just an unwritten rule. But the two of you..." Juno smiled, then shook her head. "Catriona has her hands full with the two of you."

Ariana wondered if that might be the reason she could be returning to the fae world, if she was. That Catriona wanted to separate them. But Ariana couldn't imagine that Catriona would release her to the fae world instead of just telling her and Malik that they couldn't be together.

"Can that even happen?" Xalta sounded skeptical.

"Something strange is happening to me." Ariana spread her wings and wrapped them around herself. Would she miss them? Probably. They were handy to have when she needed to rescue people over land or water that contained iron ore and she could fly when they couldn't transport in the fae way. Would she miss the job? She did love the whole concept of saving people and teaching them to be more careful in the future. She did like how she could be invisible around the fae, which she couldn't be if she was one of the fae again. It was great for eavesdropping. She, like others of their kind, could eavesdrop invisibly on humans, sure, but not on their own kind.

But most of all, she didn't want to leave Malik behind. What if her mind was wiped of everything that had happened if she was returned? Then again, everyone knew the angels had saved them and they hadn't had their minds wiped of the knowledge.

"Well, the biggest thing is whether Catriona's going to let us finish this mission when it has nothing to do with saving someone," Juno said, lying down on her bed and pulling the blue quilt over her.

"We're saving Tully's men from the dragon fae's dungeon, if we can." Ariana laid back down.

"I heard the dragon fae say that they would give Tully's men jobs. Maybe Ferdinand is working instead of being incarcerated," Xalta said.

There was a problem with that assumption. The men on the ship were trying to get Ariana safely to the mainland to escape Tully. The men the dragon fae had captured in the woods had been guards and such working for Tully when he had captured Princess Esmeralda.

Xalta cleared her throat. "Do you believe the assassin fae's story?"

"I do."

Juno scoffed. "I'd want to terminate him myself."

"What did you do before you came to be an angel?" Ariana asked her.

"I was a gardener and tended all the flowers. I set fresh flowers in the royal family's chambers every day—which is why I was accused of stealing jewelry, which wasn't so."

"Okay, I understand now. That makes sense," Ariana said.

Everyone grew quiet after that and they finally fell asleep and then in the morning, they woke so they could eat and be on their way. When Ariana climbed out of bed, both Juno and Xalta were staring at her.

"What?"

"Your wings are gone," Juno said. "Your fae aura is completely visible."

Ariana tried to make her wings reveal themselves, but it was like in the beginning when she couldn't make them appear. She attempted to turn invisible so that Xalta couldn't see her, but she was watching Ariana the whole time. Okay, so this really didn't mean Ariana was a fae again, did it?

Ariana transported to the great hall. At least she could still transport as a fae, or angel.

Malik and Elwin joined her. Malik looked distraught. Even Elwin appeared... uncomfortable.

"What's wrong?" Other than Ariana had no angel wings this morning.

"We've been recalled. Catriona's learned you're safe on the mainland. You no longer need our assistance," Malik said, taking hold of her hand with tenderness. There was something deeper going on here. Something more profound.

"But what about Xalta and Ferdinand? What about Tully and Faraday?" Ariana should have realized they would have no say in any further fae matters that didn't have anything to do with guardian angel quests. She hadn't wanted to believe it was true. She desperately wanted to help Tully's men.

"You..."—Malik choked on the word, and she swore his eyes

were misty with tears—"sorry, you're free to go. To do whatever you wish with your life as a fae."

She couldn't help but just stare at Malik. She heard, but she truly hadn't heard what he'd said as if every thought rushing through her mind had all become scrambled. "But what about..." She glanced at Elwin, wishing he'd get a clue and give them some privacy, but he only shoved his hands in his pockets and watched them, as if he was ensuring Malik got his point across sufficiently. *Fine.*

She grabbed Malik's free arm and transported him to the guest chamber she had spent the night in. Granted the room was in the women's wing, but the ladies had already left.

"What about us?" she asked Malik, tears filling her eyes. Why couldn't she have her life back and Malik in it?

"It's not meant to be. It was..." He took a deep breath, his hands on her arms, rubbing them gently. "It just was never meant to be."

She didn't believe that. Life couldn't be this cruel. "Because you couldn't get your nerve up to talk to me when we were still both fae?"

"I'm an angel. You're fae. You're special. I'm not. It means you need to return to your life and live it to the fullest, but don't put yourself at unnecessary risk."

"Because my guardian angel might not be there when I need him."

"I'll always regret that I didn't rescue you that day," Malik said.

"Don't ever regret it. I would never have met the man I'd fall in love with." Because Ariana had. Malik was sweet and caring, in charge, yet let her take charge when he knew she needed to. He was as protective of her as she felt of him.

She kissed him, wanting to transport him far away from Catriona where she could never give him another mission. But just as he deepened the kiss, his beautiful wings wrapped around her in a protective, endearing embrace, he was gone.

She was staring at the space before her, wondering what had

happened. Had he left her because he couldn't stand the thought of prolonging saying goodbye? He hadn't even told her he loved her too. But she knew he did. Even if he wouldn't say it. Even if he couldn't say it.

Tears rolled down her cheeks and she couldn't stop them if she'd tried. Xalta burst into the room, then seeing her, stopped dead in her tracks. "You're…you're still here."

"I'm a hawk fae and no longer an angel."

"Oh, oh, I'm so glad." Xalta gave her a big hug. "Don't you see? Tully and Faraday will no longer want you. You're safe now. Come, eat with us. The queen will want to know that you're still here. Both Elwin and Juno told her goodbye, but neither you nor Malik had. I…I hoped you would still be here. Once we eat, Halloran wants us to get on our way."

"The others have gone?" Ariana felt like her thoughts were still so muddled.

"Aye, they are. They said duty calls. Their mission here was done. One minute they were there and then the next"—Xalta snapped her fingers—"they were gone."

Ariana felt numb. She didn't remember going to the great hall where everyone was busy talking and eating or even sitting down beside the queen.

The queen leaned over at one point and patted her arm. "Ritasia will be delighted once you have returned to the hawk fae kingdom. And so will Princess Esmeralda. The king as well. And I'm sure your father will be overjoyed to learn you are safe and well. But if you don't have a job to return to, you may always work for me."

"Thank you, Your Majesty."

But nothing would be the same for Ariana without her mentor and her friend who had captured her heart. She couldn't believe he had wanted to be her friend so badly before they'd both become angels. She was being selfish though. He wanted to continue to be an angel—and he didn't have a choice anyway. She had wanted more than anything to be fae again. They both had gotten what they had wanted, so why did she feel so dispirited? So miserable?

After they broke their fast, Ariana and the dragon fae thanked their hosts for the meals, camaraderie, clothes, and accommodations. And then they headed out. The dragon fae kingdom was too far north for them to transport all the way. They would have to travel in stages, rest up at other kingdoms along the way, or journey by flying with the dragons or walking through the forests, which wouldn't be as safe, not with Tully or other brigands on the loose. Though with a dragon escort, once they shifted, the odds would change in their favor quickly enough.

Ariana suspected Halloran was itching to run into the duke on a forest hike.

Once they could transport no more, they made camp to eat the nooning meal. Xalta stayed close to Ariana at all times. Ariana suspected Xalta felt safer being close to her. Maybe because Ariana had been trained as a royal guard, even if she was no longer a guardian angel.

Rex, the dark fae assassin, was nearby, watching her, as if he meant to protect her just in case Claude somehow learned she was alive and returning home and wanted to have her eliminated still. She appreciated it.

"Do you think they'd take you back if you were saving someone and died while doing so?" Xalta asked as she sat next to Ariana on a log next to the campfire at the meal.

"You mean the Angel Corp? I wouldn't bet on it." Ariana figured she'd had one chance to prove herself as being worthy to serve as an angel and she had proved unworthy. She couldn't help feeling so conflicted. For a while, she truly had been special. People had looked at her in disbelief and awe when they saw her angelic, white, feathery wings. Now? She was just one of the fae again.

As a royal guard among the hawk fae, she had a position of

power and prestige. But here, among the dragon fae, she was nobody. Just a fae. And when she returned to the hawk fae kingdom, she might not be one of the royal guard again either. Had she made a mistake in wanting to return to the fae world so badly?

"I know how you feel," Xalta said. "I mean, not about the angel part of it, but about how you feel concerning Malik. That's how I am about Ferdinand."

"You would do anything to get him released from the dragon fae's dungeon if he's incarcerated," Ariana said.

"Aye, I would."

Which gave Ariana the same notion. She would do the same for Malik, except he wasn't in a fae-bound situation. He was an angel who didn't want the same thing as her.

She sighed, needing to get with the program here. She had work to do, even if it didn't have anything to do with her job back in the hawk fae kingdom, or angel business.

She had to make a plan. First, she was helping free Ferdinand and the other men if she could. Then she was returning to the hawk fae kingdom to see her father. She would see Charity and Esmeralda and learn how the princess was faring after her ordeal. Ariana would visit with Queen Ritasia and King Tiernan and hope she would get her job back. If she couldn't, she'd come up with another plan.

After they ate, Halloran decided they would walk through the woods for a while. Tully's people weren't happy with the prospect, worried, she was sure, that they would come across Duke Tully, and he would want to terminate them for helping to free her from the island. Running into Duke Tully would suit Halloran just fine because he'd take the duke prisoner and make him pay for all his crimes.

Duke Tully's men had to rely on the help of the dragons though, both as escort when they had to be on the ground, and with flying, when the dragons decided to carry them that way from high above the trees until they could all rest up from fae transportation.

They'd walked for about five miles, and Ariana was ready to transport to the next place that they could. Her feet were killing her. If Halloran didn't want to transport, afraid he'd miss finding Tully, the dragons could fly and carry the rest of them and look for Tully that way.

* * *

MALIK HAD FIGURED he and Ariana would be in trouble with Catriona for making mistakes in the situation with Duke Tully. But he'd never thought she would send Ariana back to the fae world as a fae. He felt terrible that he hadn't been able to tell Ariana he loved her too before he was rudely yanked back to the angel realm. As soon as he was there, he was standing outside Catriona's office, and he knew that meant she wanted to see him right away. He wondered if Juno and Elwin had already reported on what had gone down while dealing with Tully and the repercussions they'd faced.

Catriona's assistant said, "She's waiting for you. Go right in. And, uh, don't ask any questions."

Like why Ariana had returned to the fae world?

"You wanted to see me?" Malik asked, entering Catriona's office quickly.

"Aye. You have a new assignment."

He prayed he wasn't being given a new angel to mentor. He'd taken care of several new angels, even Juno when she'd first come here. But after being Ariana's mentor, he didn't want to be anyone else's. What was up with that? He generally liked the job, unless Elwin was interfering with his mentor's assignments like he had with Ariana.

"You have to save this woman," Catriona said, giving him a mission in Tucson, Arizona.

He desperately wanted to ask her about Ariana, but she motioned to him. "Go. Time is of the essence."

He left Catriona's office and found Elwin and Juno first in the dining hall. "I've got to go, but once I've finished the mission—"

"You're going to find Ariana," Elwin said.

"Yeah."

"We'll cover for you," Elwin said.

Juno nodded. "We will."

"Okay, I'll be back when I can." Then he transported to Tucson, to the place where he was supposed to be and found the woman in question. She was coming out of a bar, inebriated already and it was only four in the afternoon. "Ma'am, you'll need to take a taxi or Uber home. You've had too much to drink."

The woman was only in her twenties, and she only smiled at him. She didn't heed his warning. As soon as she got into her car, he was in it too and took her car keys from her. "No driving. I can take you there myself if you need me to."

"Give me my keys back," she said, angrily and tried to snatch them away from him.

He took her hand and pulled her into his arms. He normally was a lot more chivalrous on a job, but he couldn't focus. All he wanted to do was be with Ariana, to make sure she remained safe, especially now that she was fae again and could be hurt. He knew he needed to do what was right as an angel, but he just couldn't when his mind was on Ariana.

Then he transported the woman to her home. She was staring at him in disbelief and the fae transportation had totally disoriented her. He took her inside her house. Then he showed off his wings. Her eyes widened.

"I'm your guardian angel but for late this afternoon only. After that, you're on your own."

The woman sat down hard on her couch and then Malik left. They didn't always have someone record their work and he was glad this time he hadn't. Then he returned to the fae world and began looking for Ariana, the subject of his desire. She was everything to him and he didn't want to ever give her up.

He searched a long time for her and hoped he'd find her before Catriona learned he'd finished his assignment and then she'd give him another. Not that they always had another one right away. Which was another reason he was trying to find Ariana as soon as he could.

But everywhere he looked, he couldn't locate her. Then he finally saw her hawk fae trail on a forest path headed in a different direction than he'd thought they would go and he was overjoyed to locate her.

He finally saw her up ahead on the pine tree path, walking alongside Xalta. She was safe and he couldn't have been any gladder to see her.

CHAPTER 14

$\mathcal{B}$efore Ariana could suggest that Halloran and the other dragons fly and carry people for a while because her feet needed a rest, she felt a hand on her shoulder. Xalta gave a startled scream, and Ariana's first thought was it was Tully, and she whipped around to see who was touching her.

Malik.

She took a relieved breath and smiled. His wings were on full display as if he was showing off to her and she was cheered at once to see him. She quickly gave him a warm embrace.

He smiled broadly at her. "I had to return to tell you I love you." Then he took hold of her hand as everyone watched them, and he and she proceeded to walk.

"I love you too. You vanished on me," she said.

"I was pulled away against my will. I have to admit I had ignored Catriona's repeated calls to return to angel headquarters."

"Oh, Malik, I don't want to get you into trouble. Why are you here now?"

"I just finished a mission, and I was in the vicinity, so I wanted to check on you and make sure you're okay."

She didn't believe it and gave him a look like she didn't.

He smiled. "Okay, I wasn't exactly in the vicinity but close enough."

She gave him another look of disbelief.

He chuckled. "All right. I've been traveling for hours looking for you. You're off the beaten path that I thought you would have taken to the dragon fae territory."

"Halloran wanted to see if he could find any sign of Tully." She pulled Malik to a stop and hugged him tightly. "I don't want to lose you. I know I'm being selfish, but that's how I feel."

He sighed and kissed her. "You're not losing me, as long as you don't mind having an angel for a boyfriend."

"As long as you don't get into trouble for it, I'm all for it."

"It means I can be called back to do a mission at any time. But when I don't have one, I'm coming to see you."

"And you won't be in trouble for it." She wanted to make sure that he wasn't going to be hurt over this. Otherwise, she was willing to do anything to be with him whenever he could get away.

"I want to be with you." He didn't say anything about not getting into trouble for it.

For now, she was really glad he was here with her. "Does anyone know you're here with me?" She thought it would be a bad sign if he was keeping his actions secret from everyone, including his friends.

"Yeah. Juno and Elwin. I almost didn't tell Elwin, afraid he'd snitch, but he said he understood how I felt, and he was all for covering for me if I needed him to."

"Wow, okay. I never thought he would go against the rules to help anyone else out." She really was surprised. "Though I guess dumping me in the ocean to rescue the paddler during a storm wasn't exactly following the rules. And he thought it would help me to go on more advance assignments." She hadn't been sure about his motives there. "Did Catriona say anything about me?"

Ariana really wanted to know why she had been released as an angel and returned to the fae realm.

"She didn't say anything about anything. She just put me to work."

"You didn't ask?"

Malik shook his head as she and he began to walk with the others again. "You know Catriona. If she wants you to know something, she'll tell you. Otherwise, you don't ask."

True. Ariana had learned that from her own experience, though she thought Catriona might have said something to Malik about why she wasn't an angel any longer.

"Can you carry me for a while?" she asked.

Malik looked down at her.

She shrugged. "If I had angel wings, I'd fly myself. My feet are hurting, and Halloran won't fly us, and he doesn't want us to transport someplace else without an escort."

"Because he wants to keep looking for the duke."

"Right."

Malik wrapped his arms around her and flew overhead.

The dragon fae all looked up at them and shortly after that, the dragons gave Duke Tully's men and Xalta a lift and they flew for miles before they were ready to transport to the next location.

Again, they stopped for a meal in the woods, glad Queen Irenis had sent enough food for them to last for the first day's journey.

But then they heard someone in the woods, and Halloran and some of his men went to investigate. Ariana was curious and wanted to check out what was going on too, but she didn't want to leave Malik for a second in the event he was suddenly called away to save someone. She would never forgive herself if she didn't say goodbye to him. Who knew when she would be able to see him again?

He knew her well enough that he took her with him to check

things out. "Thank you." That's when they saw two of the duke's men trying to escape the dragons, both men wearing iron bracelets, preventing them from transporting. But the dragons quickly shifted and caught them.

"What happened here?" Halloran asked the men.

Obviously, the duke's men hadn't done this to themselves.

"Duke Tully's men are mutinying because he'd taken the angel hostage." The one man looked over and saw Malik carrying Ariana to the scene. "Her," he said, pointing to Ariana. "How... how did you escape the island?"

"Some of Duke Tully's men helped me escape. Halloran is helping them reach the dragon fae kingdom to find new jobs," Ariana said.

The two men smiled. "We're ready for new employment. Can you remove these?" They showed them their iron bracelets.

"When we reach the dragon fae castle, we can remove the manacles," Halloran said. "Come with us." He took one of the men, and another dragon took the other. "Where is Duke Tully?"

"He left. He heard the two of us talking about doing wrong by the angel, and he left us here for being disloyal. He figured we'd die in the woods, that no one would come across us before it was too late, but we planned to walk until we came to a village, and then we heard voices in that direction," the one man said, waving an arm toward Halloran's camp. "We were afraid it might be highway robbery men."

"But then we saw the dragons and we figured we were really done for," the other man said.

When they reached the camp, the duke's men looked up to see their friends arriving with the dragons. They greeted them and Ariana was thinking that Duke Tully was having a revolt on his hands, all because of her. That was one time that his hostage taking had really backfired on him.

She smiled. Maybe her saving Duke Tully hadn't been such a bad thing after all. Maybe in this way, he would have to change his ways. Now she was helping to free the men who worked for him on that hidden Mystic Island.

"Where is the duke?" Halloran asked the men. "Did he mention where he was headed next?"

"No. He never does. We just always have had to follow him where he wanted to go. He never gave us a heads-up. Now with this business with Ariana, he's really spooked," the one man said.

"Good," Ariana said.

"How did you get free? The duke was talking about how worried he was about leaving you behind because he was afraid that his wizard would try and grab you. But he was also concerned about bringing you with him because you could leave us and maybe even get him in trouble with the Angel Corp for holding you hostage. He was so distracted, he wasn't even paying attention to travelers passing on the road, one of whom was a wealthy merchant," the one man said. "We didn't mention it to him because we figured we're all in enough hot water as it is."

"We took her in the boat," one of the men who helped her and Xalta escape the island said. "But things weren't easy for us. The weather was bad, and our boat capsized. Luckily, we were far enough away from the island that Ariana could use her wings to ferry us to the dark fae mainland."

The two men looked astonished. "We didn't have any choice about leaving with the duke last night," the one man said. "We've all been talking about it when the duke's not around."

Brett was quiet up until this point and he finally said, "What about this Faraday? I've never heard of him."

The men exchanged glances. "He's powerful. That's all we know. We don't have any idea what kind of fae he is. He hides his aura."

"Yeah, and though he works with Duke Tully, he doesn't like it when the duke thinks the wizard actually works for him. We know the wizard in the hawk fae realm actually works for King

Tiernan," the other man said. "But you're the one who doesn't work for the dragon fae queen. You're your own man, correct?"

"That's true," Brett said. He was both phantom fae and dragon fae and he was now mated to Ena. He would do whatever he could to help the dragon fae kingdom though. And others, if they were allied with the dragon fae.

But Ariana knew he was also loyal to the phantom fae.

"Thank you for giving safe passage to the dragon fae kingdom," one of the new men said.

"Aye, thanks. The duke left us to perish," the other man said.

And so why had she had to save Duke Tully?

Then they all headed out again.

"So what was your mission?" she asked Malik, walking beside him, hand in hand.

He explained about the drunk woman. "She was young and has her whole life ahead of her." Truly, he wasn't sure why he had been sent on the mission to save the woman. At times like this, he really wanted to know. Maybe she impacted on the fae in some way later that would have dire consequences to his people? He didn't know.

"What are we going to do about us?" she asked.

"I don't know. I'm going to be here, seeing you as much as I can. But you're going to be working too, once you return to the hawk fae kingdom."

She worried about that, that they would drift apart. Though right now, she couldn't imagine it.

* * *

THE NEXT AFTERNOON, they finally reached the dragon fae kingdom and the first order of business was freeing Xalta's boyfriend and seeing about the others the dragons had captured.

Halloran smiled at Ariana. "They have all been released and given jobs."

153

Xalta found Ferdinand helping to rebuild a stone wall surrounding a garden. But as soon as he saw her, Xalta and Ferdinand rejoiced with the warm reunion. Ariana was about ready to get on with other matters, when Xalta ran to hug her. "Thank you."

"And thank *you*. I couldn't have left the island without your help."

"The men were going to take you with or without me."

Ariana gave her a hug back and then Xalta left her to be with Ferdinand.

The woman in the cottage came out and welcomed Xalta, then the two of them began working in the garden. Ariana was relieved to see Xalta would have a place here also. Then Ariana and the others had a big celebration with the royalty here too. It was so much fun. She hadn't expected it, but she was really delighted that Malik was there to enjoy it too, and that he hadn't been called away yet. He deserved the accolades just like the other angels did for helping to rescue the others. And she'd been thrilled they'd come out to assist them too.

But just as they sat down at the high table with the queen and other dignitaries, Malik sighed and gave her a kiss. "I've got to go."

"No."

"Yeah, sorry. Duty calls. Again." Malik gave her a big hug. "But I want to be with you when you reach the hawk fae kingdom."

"I'll be staying with the phantom fae first, and then we'll cross No Man's Land to reach the hawk fae kingdom."

"If I can, I'll take you there myself from the phantom fae kingdom."

"But if you can't, Brett will take me." She was hoping that Malik would come for her, but if he couldn't, she would go with Brett. She couldn't always rely on Malik to do what he said he hoped to do, as much as she wished he could be there with her. It wasn't just that she felt he would protect her, but that she wanted him to meet her father.

He kissed her quickly goodbye, and she really hated that he had to leave like this, and she gave him a deeper kiss until he vanished into thin air.

Ugh!

Ena came over and gave her a hug. "I'm so sorry that the two of you are separated between realms like this."

"Yeah, me too."

Ena sighed. "Well, since you and Brett will be going to the phantom fae kingdom tomorrow, we want you to stay with us at our castle tonight."

"Of course, I want to." The queen's castle was really nice, but Ariana had gotten to know Ena better and she loved the idea of staying with her and Brett.

She noticed Halloran offering to put Rex up for the night.

* * *

LATE THAT EVENING, Ariana settled down in one of the guest chambers when she heard pounding at the front door of the keep. "Coming! Coming!" Ryder, the butler, called out, sounding highly irritated. The door opened.

"Is Ariana here? I followed her dust trail here."

Malik! He'd returned for her! She couldn't believe it and jumped out of bed, throwing a cloak over her shift.

"Oh, aye, come in. I will talk to the lady and let her know." The butler walked through the castle, but Ariana practically flew out of the guest chamber to be with Malik.

Upon seeing Ariana rushing through the hall in her exuberance, the butler gasped. "I was going to make sure it was all right with Ena."

"It's all right. She will approve." Ariana threw herself into

Malik's arms. "You know, we're going to have to do something about Catriona separating us all the time."

Malik chuckled and ran his hands through Ariana's hair. "Do you mind if we get some rest? I'm afraid I'll be called on at any time."

"No. Let's go." She took him to her chamber, shut the door, and they climbed into bed.

"We can't...do anything," he warned.

"I know. You're an angel."

He smiled and kissed her. "I don't feel really angelic right now."

"Good, because I don't want you to be."

He snuggled with her, and she hoped he wouldn't be called away in the middle of the night. Though she did have the notion that if he started to cross No Man's Land with her and he suddenly was made to take an assignment, that could be dangerous for her. Brett would still have to come with them. And Ena said she would too.

Ariana woke later that morning to find Malik gone, and she groaned. Had he tried to wake her before he left? Or had he just vanished so he could take care of business and return to her as soon as possible? She sure didn't like this part of the bargain, though she had to remind herself at least she had this much with him.

* * *

MALIK KNEW this was going to be a tough proposition, him coming and going all the time. And he was certain Catriona would get wind of it and be upset with him before too much longer. An angel was supposed to be sleeping in his room, not sleeping with a fae in the fae world.

Catriona had summoned him so he had to go to her office

right away. When he went in to see her, she said, "Your room has not been slept in."

He needed to remedy that whenever he planned to spend the night with Ariana. He didn't tell Catriona why he had not been in his room last night. For all he knew, she was already well aware of what was going on.

"I have a mission for you. I'm sure you know that Ariana is trying to return to her home in the hawk fae kingdom. She will meet some resistance. You'll need to see that she gets there safely. I didn't release her just to have her die on us."

He opened his mouth to speak, to tell Catriona he would guard Ariana with his life and not make the same mistake twice.

But Catriona raised her hand to silence him before he could get a word out. "A fae and an angel cannot be together. I'm sure you understand this. It's not something we normally speak to our Angel Corp members about. It's just…a given. Go, protect her."

"I will." Then he left to see Elwin and Juno before he went to take care of Ariana. He relished the idea he could be there with her, by Catriona's orders even. "Hey, Elwin, I've got a mission to save Ariana."

Elwin laughed.

"I'm serious."

"I know you are but…forget it. I'm coming with you. I might get called on to go on another case in the meantime, but if Ariana needs us, I'm going with you," Elwin said.

Malik was surprised, but glad Elwin wanted to assist them.

"We're going to get Juno too, aren't we? She'll be an angelic terror if she's left out," Elwin said.

"Yeah sure." If she wanted to come.

They went to Juno's room next and knocked on the door.

"This better be a life-or-death matter," Juno called out grumpily.

"Ariana needs us," Malik said.

"Sanctioned? Forget it. It doesn't matter. I'm coming."

Malik smiled at Elwin. All three of them had been good about toeing the line. But once Ariana had showed up? All bets were off.

Then Juno opened her door, pulled on her boots, and went with them. "Okay, so what's the deal? Ariana is in trouble again?"

"Yeah, and Catriona actually sanctioned it," Elwin said. "Wonders never cease."

Then they transported to Ena and Brett's castle. He hoped they wouldn't be upset that they were returning at this time of night. One of the guards on the wall walk came down to open the gate. "It's kind of late, isn't it?"

But they all spread out their angel wings and he immediately let them in. It was kind of neat really that they were treated like royalty. The butler let them into the castle next, and he was shaking his head. "Don't you angels ever sleep?"

"We intend to. We just need a room to sleep in," Elwin said. "Malik and I will share one. Juno can stay with Ariana."

"You and Juno can share a chamber. I'm staying with Ariana," Malik said.

Juno folded her arms. "I'm *not* staying with Elwin."

The butler let out his breath. "I'll take the two of you to separate chambers. Malik, you know the way to Ariana's room."

Malik left his friends and knocked at Ariana's door, but she didn't answer him. He didn't want to disturb her, so he let himself in and joined her in bed.

"Ohmigoddess, you've returned," she said, hugging him to pieces.

This was the warm welcome he was truly glad for. "Always. Catriona has made me your protector to ensure you arrive home safely. Elwin and Juno came too."

Ariana smiled and cuddled against him. "Good."

They kissed and then they slept for the rest of the night before they had breakfast with the staff and Ena and Brett. Then they headed for the phantom fae kingdom and Brett's earlier home. The butler had told Ena and Brett that they had additional angel company that night, so when they gathered in the dining hall, they weren't surprised to see the extra mouths to feed.

"So the head of the angels said you needed to protect Ariana? What's supposed to happen?" Ena asked.

"We never really know for sure," Malik said. "But crossing No Man's Land can be a challenge. Though we'll be flying overhead and hopefully we won't have any trouble."

"Should we contact my brother to go with us?" Ena asked. "Halloran would come with us in a heartbeat, if we needed him to."

"I think we'll be covered, but if he wants to come, sure, that's fine with us," Malik said. More dragons would be a welcome sight. Anyone would, who could help to keep Ariana safe.

"So your boss okayed this then?" Ena said, sounding amused.

"Well, Malik's being here, yes. We're here to help, but if we are called, we'll have to leave," Juno said. "Though we won't want to."

"Right," Elwin said. "All for one and one for all."

Malik had been friends with Elwin and Juno before Ariana had joined them, but he had never expected her to bring them closer together like this.

One of the men working for Ena and Brett left the table and within the hour, Halloran and three of their dragon friends and Rex joined them for breakfast.

"Well, I didn't think we'd get back with all of you so soon, if ever. But we'd do anything to help Ariana get home safely," Halloran said.

"Well, thanks," Ariana said. "I sure appreciate everyone's help."

Once they were ready, they headed out, the dragons flying, the angels flying, and Malik was glad to have Ariana in his arms for a little while longer.

As soon as they arrived at the phantom fae castle, they were again greeted with fanfare. Ariana was used to the royal family being regarded in that way when she accompanied them, but she wasn't the one they regaled in that way. So it was all new to her that an angel, or former angel, would be treated like that. She hadn't thought she would relish it as much as she did, more used to keeping a low profile so she could protect the royals.

Word had already reached them about the angels escorting a former angel to the hawk fae kingdom across No Man's Land. Most had never seen an angel before. And never one who had been an angel and then one of the fae again.

"I'm eager to talk to King Tiernan's mage to learn if he knows anything about Faraday," Brett said. "Eleron knows how to do a lot of things I don't."

That was still something that Malik had wanted to do. Learn a way to eliminate Faraday, and maybe the magic that was being used to hide Mystic Island would vanish. Then Duke Tully could easily be captured. And the people living on the island could live their lives out from under the wizard's influence and the duke's illegal activities.

Maybe even those who were going to be employed by the dragons could return to their island home. Not that Catriona would allow the angels to try and take down a wizard. And not that they could do anything about a powerful wizard either.

"You know you could check with the falcon fae also. They have some powerful magic users," Ena said.

If they could unite some of the mages, no matter how powerful Faraday was, they should stand a chance to defeat him.

CHAPTER 15

*E*arly that morning, Brett and Ena, Halloran, and their three dragon friends shifted into dragons. Malik unfolded his wings and carried Ariana, and Juno and Elwin were nearby as they all flew over the dangerous desert of No Man's Land. Brett carried Rex. As soon as they began to cross the desert, sandworms, twenty feet in length, erupted out of the fine sandy soil, swinging their heads at the dragons and Malik and Ariana and the other angels. The sandworms' jagged, multi-rows of teeth were fully bared as they snapped at them, trying to reach them as they flew overhead. The sandworms could feel vibrations if anyone walked across the sand dunes, but also the dragons' and angels' wings flapping overhead sent vibrations through the air, impacting lightly on the white sand, enough to alert the giant sandworms.

Whirling sand devils like small tornadoes whipped about, sandblasting everything in their path. They popped up randomly, so there wasn't any way to predict them and in one minute, blowing sand was shifting about, and then the next minute a funnel formed, sweeping whoever happened to be there up in it. As soon as one enveloped Malik and Adriana in a funnel, he fought against the winds to fly straight through the wind devil, but the strong, circulating winds were making it difficult. Suddenly, Halloran dove underneath him and carried him and Ariana through the funnel. With Halloran's leathery wings, they were much better suited to getting through a blast of sand than feathery wings.

Malik could barely see through the sand scouring them, but then he felt a hot burst of flame nearby and glanced to his left. Ena was shooting a steady hot blue flame, striking a sandworm that had whipped around to bite at her, but her dragon flame took him out and he fell to the sand dunes and disappeared beneath the sand.

Halloran, Malik, and Ariana finally broke through the funnel, hoping that they wouldn't run into another before they crossed the sand dunes to the mountain range.

Sheer mountains of granite rock were straight ahead, and a narrow passage was visible, known as the Salt Canyon because the white sand walls looked like salt. One of the dragons even kept her gold in one of the caves in the mountains, safe from anyone who wanted to pilfer it because of all the deadly creatures living there and the inaccessibility. Dragons usually didn't have to worry about other dragons stealing their gold. They earned enough on taking quests for people who had no way of solving them without the dragons' help. They headed for Salt Canyon, just missing another blast of a funnel that had erupted.

An old-growth pine forest grew beyond the mountain range and wraithlike creatures were known to frequent the area, floating on the breeze, killing anything they could reach. And a blue crystal lake nearby was filled with *aughisky*. They were shapeshifting fae, sometimes appearing in the form of water ponies, water spirits, that attacked all living things that tried to swim in their lake and ripped them to shreds to nice bitesize pieces before eating them.

Once they made it through the woods, the land turned into a

lush green meadow, and crystal blue lakes dotted the area. They were safe now.

Way ahead, they saw the castle spires of the hawk fae kingdom, King Tiernan's, hawks embroidered on each of the flags of the five towers, announcing Ariana was home.

The dragons had built smaller castles of their own here when they had been banished from their own kingdom until they could return and set the right queen on the throne, so now they used the castles during visits to the kingdom. A couple of the dragons used their castles as a place to store their gold also and hired hawk fae to guard it. No one would be crazy enough to try and steal from them though.

When they finally reached the hawk fae kingdom, Ariana and Malik went straight to her father's cottage to tell him she was alive and well, while Juno and Elwin were seeing the sights in the hawk fae kingdom. Of course Ariana wanted to tell the king herself that Claude was the one who tried to have her eliminated and not King Tiernan on the hunt, but she knew Claude wasn't interested in killing the king, so he was safe. And she wanted to see her father first. In the meantime, Rex was staying with Halloran at his castle until they needed him.

Ariana was excited, but worried, not wanting to give her father a heart attack when he saw her. But he wasn't home, surprising her. He'd been a royal guard before he retired and now he was working his little farm, taking care of black-faced sheep and goats and chickens, just what he'd always wanted to do.

She noticed the goats and sheep were gone and she figured he had taken them to the pastureland north of here. "Come on. Let's head up the trail to the pastureland. I see his recent fae dust trail here. I'm sure that's where he's gone."

"Are you sure it's okay with your dad that I stay with you at his cottage? Brett and Ena will put us up at their castle, if not."

She smiled. "Are you worried my father will object to you being here with me?"

Malik chuckled. "Yeah, who knows how he'll react."

"He'll be thrilled. Remember, he has had a ton of guardian angel saves so he knows how important you are. And if the two of you don't get along, we'll stay at one of the dragons' castles. I was living at the royal castle because I was on-call all the time, so I won't be able to return there unless I'm working as a royal guard again."

"So you'll be staying with your dad from now on?"

"Until I can have a cottage of my own built on the property. That way I can be near to his place too and help my father, but at the same time be able to live my own life."

"Especially if you have a boyfriend who has erratic visiting hours."

"I'll say."

They started walking up the trail and she heard her father talking to the animals like he always did. Then she smiled and took Malik's hand in hers. "I don't want to scare him."

"Maybe he got word already. It's amazing how fast word travels throughout the kingdoms."

That was certainly true. "Dad!" she called out to warn him she was on her way to see him. She could have transported to his location, but she figured it would be easier on him to do it this way.

Then she saw their black and white sheepdog, Rufus, guarding the sheep and goats. He bounded toward her to greet her. And she gave him a big hug.

Her father's jaw dropped. "Ohmigoddess, Ariana!" He ran to meet up with her, but then stopped dead in his tracks. "You're here to save me?" He glanced at Malik who had his wings on display.

Show off.

She hugged her father. "I love you, Dad. I hadn't said it before I left with Charity to go to South Padre Island, and I've wanted to ever since that day."

"I know. I felt the same way, and"—her father's eyes were filled with tears—"here I'd always had a guardian angel looking out for me and you should have had one taking care of you."

"I was her guardian angel, and I didn't save her," Malik said, putting his hand on Ariana's back and rubbed it. "It was my fault."

"He was trying to save someone else. But I'm back now for good." She smiled at her father and hugged him again. "I'm no longer an angel. I don't know why exactly. I wanted to return to the fae world no matter what, and I planned to find a way to do it. Then the next thing I know I'm here and a fae again."

"With your guardian angel." Her father frowned at Malik. "Are you here to apologize?"

"No, he was serving as my guardian angel to reach you safely and protected me this time. But he and I are dating."

Her father's eyes widened, and he glanced back at Malik. "Are you serious? Can you even do that?"

She shrugged. "We are."

"Well, come on. Let's get the animals back to the cottage before it gets any later. Can you stay and eat with us?" her father asked Malik.

"He's staying overnight, unless he gets called to go on a mission." That was one thing she was concerned about. He'd already accomplished his mission, so now he was free to be called upon to do another angel quest at any time.

Her father again looked from Ariana to Malik. "At my place?"

"If it's a problem, we'll stay at one of the dragons' castles."

"No, no, oh, no. I wouldn't have it any other way. You both stay with me. Malik can sleep on the couch."

Her father had only two bedrooms in the small cottage, but she wasn't having Malik sleep on the couch. She hoped her father would be fine with it.

"I can't believe you're home and safe and a fae again. We've heard everything about you being an angel and coming to

Princess Esmeralda's help. And then that Duke Tully had taken you prisoner."

As Rufus herded the sheep and goats home, she told her father all that had happened.

"Thank the goddess for you being freed then. And Duke Tully?" her father asked.

"Everyone's searching for him. No one suspected that he'd take Ariana, an angel, hostage," Malik said. "Not only that, but his wizard wanted her for his own."

"Well, an angel could be useful. I've sure needed them over the years," her father said.

"Until you started being more careful," she said.

"Yeah, I finally realized I was not immortal. And neither are you, Daughter."

She smiled. "Yeah, like I found out."

Then they reached home, and they planned to have a simple dinner before she and Rex told him about Claude, but King Tiernan's mage showed up at the house instead and he bowed low.

"King Tiernan requests your presence for dinner—a celebration for the both of you saving his sister from Duke Tully. And of course, your father is his honored guest for raising such a great royal guard to take his place when he retired," Eleron said.

"Is my position taken?" she asked.

"Uh, you were gone. And then you were an angel. So yes, Claude took your position."

"Claude?" She couldn't believe it! That's why he had wanted her out of the way in the first place. Not because he was livid about her dumping him, but because he wanted her job!

"I'm sure the king will consider giving you another important position for your loyalty to the royal family."

She needed to speak to the king first about this business with Claude hiring the assassin.

As soon as they entered the castle, the royal family wanted a private audience with Ariana. She wished Malik could go with her, but the invitation was only for her. Instead, he gave her a hug and kiss and went to join his friends.

She wondered if he felt more comfortable with them now, especially since he wasn't a hawk fae when most of the men and women were. Except of course for their dragon fae protectors.

"I need to bring a dark fae with me to tell the king some important news," she told the king's advisor.

He shook his head. "First, the king has business with you. Then we'll see about the dark fae."

She let out her breath in a huff. *Fine.*

On the way to the throne room, she saw Charity in the hall, and they gave each other hugs.

"I've heard the news! I can't believe you died, became an angel, and then returned to us. What did you do right? Or...uhm, wrong?" Charity asked.

Ariana laughed. "I'm so glad to see you too! I'm not sure. I did some things right, probably more things wrong. But I'm so thrilled to be here again."

"I saw the angel with you. I...uh, remember seeing him watching you at South Padre Island. I didn't know he was an angel back then."

"And you didn't tell me?" Ariana frowned at her friend.

Charity shrugged. "He was a phantom fae at the time. I didn't think you would be interested in him."

Ariana sighed. She couldn't believe her best friend had known of his interest in her before he was even an angel and Ariana had been clueless!

Charity's cheeks blushed a bit when she said, "I saw you kissing him. I didn't know an angel could kiss a fae, but I guess since you were an angel before—well, I swear you never kissed Claude like that."

Ariana smiled. "Malik is the only one for me. I've got to see the royal family. But we'll eat together at the celebration."

"Oh, no, not this time. They'll have you seated at the head

table. I guess you know your ex-boyfriend got your old job. I told you he was no good." Charity gave her another hug. "See you soon. You'll have to tell me about this angel of yours."

"Yeah, I heard the news, and I will tell you all about Malik." And about the rest of the news concerning Claude *after* she told the royal family. Ariana hugged her back and then continued on her way to the throne room. It wouldn't do to keep the royal family waiting.

King Tiernan, Queen Ritasia, and Princess Esmeralda were sitting on their gold-gilded thrones, seats and backs covered in red velvet as Ariana went in to see them. She wondered if the king would decide to give her job back to her, but she really didn't want it now. She wanted to spend the precious time she had with her father and Malik whenever he was able to visit her.

"By now, I'm certain you know your position on the royal guard staff has been filled," King Tiernan said.

She also knew the king could make another royal guard position if he wanted to. She opened her mouth to speak about Claude, though she really wanted Rex to be with her when she did, but the king continued speaking. One didn't interrupt the king unless he was in danger.

"Princess Esmeralda would like it if you would serve as her lady-in-waiting," King Tiernan continued.

Lady-in-waiting? Who served as a companion to a royal lady and did whatever she bid? Ariana was a well-trained fighting machine. Being a lady-in-waiting and helping Esmeralda to dress in the mornings or undress at night didn't appeal.

"Thank you for the generous offer." Ariana knew it wasn't a good idea to turn down the king's offer of a position in the royal household so freely given. Not when that would get her in his good graces, and it was something so many would love to do. "But after losing my life and then getting it back, I've decided I need to spend as much time as I can with my father. It made me realize how much I'd lost when I couldn't even return to tell him I love him."

She wasn't going to mention the part about not being able to see Malik whenever she had the opportunity, night or day. She'd be busy catering to a royal princess's needs instead.

King Tiernan inclined his head slightly, acquiescing. "I understand. I have another proposal for you."

Could she turn down two of the king's proposals and not be banished from the court? Breathe in, breathe out. It couldn't be all that bad, could it?

"You'll wed Cpt. Baldur of the griffin fae."

Ariana hadn't meant to, but she glanced sharply at Esmeralda who dearly loved the captain, though the king would not allow her to marry a ship's captain. Did he think Esmeralda might leave, defy her brother's orders, and marry the captain anyway? So if King Tiernan married the captain off to Ariana, then Esmeralda couldn't finally run off with him.

"The captain's people are no longer at war with us," the king said, as if that mattered to Ariana!

So let Esmeralda marry him then. The king and the queen had recently signed a peace treaty between the two kingdoms.

"The captain wishes to remain here with us and not return to the griffin fae island. I will allow it because he helped Esmeralda reach our kingdom past No Man's Land. To thank him, I wish to provide him with a suitable bride, and you will do nicely. I venture to say now that you have returned safely to us, you will get many offers, but none as great as this. He now commands half my fleet."

"I love Malik." There. She said it.

The king narrowed his eyes. Queen Ritasia frowned; Princess Esmeralda looked relieved.

"He is a guardian angel. The two of you can never be together, not truly," King Tiernan said, matter-of-factly.

"We will deal with it." Ariana didn't know if Malik would feel the same about her weeks, months from now, but she wasn't giving up on them and marrying some guy she wasn't interested in who wasn't interested in her either, even if the king wanted it. "Seriously, I'm just so happy to be home, to see all of you again, and I'm fine with that. I don't need you to do anything for me. I had to ensure the princess was safe and that's all that mattered to me."

Ariana never would have believed she would be put in this position of turning the king down twice.

"All right then," the king said. "I have nothing more." Then he and Queen Ritasia got up to leave and the queen winked at Ariana on the way out. That was a good sign. Queen Ritasia often had a lot of influence over her husband.

"Wait!" Ariana said, and she realized she sounded like she was desperate to say she changed her mind. The king and queen looked back at her. "Claude hired an assassin to kill me on the hunt the day I took the dark fae assassin's crimson bow away from him. He wasn't there to kill you, but me. Apparently, it was so Claude could take my place on the staff."

The king and queen frowned at her.

"Rex, the dark fae assassin, came with me to tell you the story, but your advisor said it would have to wait," Ariana continued.

King Tiernan looked at Ritasia for confirmation.

"She's right. Rex *is* a dark fae assassin with the guild back home," Ritasia said. Since she was a dark fae, she would know.

"Queen Irenis listened to his testimony. He was paid half the money Claude owed him to kill me, but once Rex saw me, he wouldn't do it," Ariana said.

Ritasia's lips parted. Then she smiled. "He's an honorable assassin." She said to their advisor, "Bring Claude and Rex to our solar at once. Guards also, and Claude is to be manacled before he learns what is about to happen to him."

"Aye, my queen." Their advisor hurried out of the throne room.

"Would you like your old position back?" the king asked, rubbing his chin in thought.

Ariana smiled. "No, Your Majesty. I truly want to work with my father."

He nodded, and then he and Queen Ritasia hurried out of the throne room to deal with Claude.

Esmeralda gave Ariana a hug. "Oh, thanks so much for not agreeing to marry the captain."

"I know how much you care for him, and I like him, certainly, but in no way do I want to marry him. As to serving as your lady-in-waiting—"

"Oh, no problem. I figured you could be my personal royal guard, but I totally understand that you wouldn't want to do it, given what you're used to working at."

"I would have loved to have done it if I hadn't wanted to be available anytime that Malik is able to see me."

Esmeralda smiled. "Okay, I totally understand that since I feel the same way about Ian, um, Cpt. Baldur."

"I can't believe your brother won't let the two of you be together. I mean, now that he's put him in charge of half his fleet even."

"My brother wants to find someone who is royal who would make an alliance with him through a royal marriage."

"Not the griffin king."

"He has been contemplating it. Sinbad seems nice, but he's *not* the captain."

"Right. Just like the captain isn't Malik."

"Exactly. I'm glad you were able to return home. I didn't think that would happen," Esmeralda said.

"Yeah, me either."

"Well, let's join everyone for the celebration. We want to thank you and Malik for coming to my aid." Esmeralda gave her another hug. She was definitely glad to see Ariana.

Ariana was glad she had told the king how she felt about

taking the job to serve Esmeralda, marrying the captain, or taking her old job back and didn't just go along with his plans so as not to upset his royal highness. Though the news she had shared with him afterward about Claude had definitely taken his mind off the other matters for the moment.

CHAPTER 16

Before Ariana rejoined Malik in the great hall, Charity met up with her. "Ohmigoddess, I can't believe Claude was behind attempting to have you assassinated! The king ordered him sent to the dungeon until he can decide how to dispose of him. I was in attendance while he made the decision, Queen Ritasia telling Tiernan she knew Rex to be honest and everything had made perfect sense."

Relieved, Ariana smiled. "Good. Claude deserves to be where he's at then. I need to catch up to Malik. Are you coming?"

"Waiting on the royal family. I still have to guard them, you know."

Ariana chuckled. "I'm glad for you." But when she rejoined Malik, he was wearing an odd expression. She couldn't figure out what was going on. "Is something wrong?"

"Brett was talking to Eleron and he said he knew Faraday. And he knew where he lived. He didn't realize that he has been hiding Duke Tully's island castle."

"Faraday protects Duke Tully, so he's just as guilty of doing the crimes," Ariana said.

"But he's truly powerful Eleron said."

"So what's going to happen then?" She didn't think Malik should be involved in trying to help take down a wizard.

"We're going to speak with the king of the griffin, Sinbad. And the falcon fae queen and king. Both are magic users. Not that they would want to get involved in this. They're all busy ruling their own kingdoms," Malik said.

"But you're not going to do anything about it, are you?"

"No. Though I want to be, just on principle. Not only is he hiding Duke Tully so the duke can get away with his crimes, but also because Faraday wanted to take *you* as his own hostage."

"But I'm no longer an angel so he's not going to be interested in me."

"I don't trust that he's changed his mind about it."

Still, Ariana didn't believe Faraday had any interest in her other than she had been a guardian angel. She explained to Malik about what the king had proposed to her—that she'd be a lady-in waiting to Princess Esmeralda—that brought a smile to his lips, and to marry the captain Esmeralda was in love with. Hearing that bit of news, Malik frowned.

"You're not going to, are you?" Malik asked, still looking perturbed.

"Be a lady-in-waiting to the princess? No."

"What about marrying Cpt. Baldur?"

"What do you think?" Ariana couldn't help but sound annoyed with Malik. She didn't give him a chance to answer. "Of course not. I had to tell him about Claude, and he threw him in the dungeon to deal with him later after Rex testified against him. Luckily, Ritasia knew all about Rex and believed his story over Claude's. But the king did offer me my old job back. I said no to that."

Malik finally released the breath he had been holding in anticipation. "Good about Claude, but about rejecting the king so many times, was he annoyed?"

"I don't believe he was happy. When the king says something, people do it. But I told him I love you and he told me we couldn't truly be together."

"He may be right," Malik said morosely.

"I'm *not* giving up on us." She poked at her boar stew, not happy with the direction the conversation was headed.

Malik sighed and rubbed her back in a comforting way. "What will your dad say about you turning your back on the king's wishes?"

"He'd better agree with me." Ariana thought her father would have her best interests at heart. At least she hoped so. She realized how quickly things could change from being the king's savior, to being his disobedient subject.

After they finished their meals, Elwin and Juno said goodbye. Ariana introduced her best friend to Malik.

Charity was all smiles, blushing furiously. Ariana swore it was because Malik was an angel and Charity was over the moon impressed.

"He's just a normal guy," Ariana said, trying to make Charity feel less self-conscious. She'd never seen her so flummoxed.

"Oh, no, he's not normal at all," Charity said, then her eyes grew big, and they laughed. "I mean, he's extraordinary."

"Thanks," Malik said, holding Ariana's hand. "She's the one who is totally extraordinary to me. It's good meeting you, Charity. I know the two of you are best of friends and I hope we can be too."

"Oh, aye, of course." Charity was still blushing like crazy.

Ariana smiled. "I'll see you as soon as I can."

Ariana and Malik went home to her father's cottage before it was too much later. But then Catriona called him with her telepathic communication before Malik could go inside with Ariana.

He groaned. "I'll be back as soon as I can."

"All right. Just tap on my window and I'll let you in." She kissed Malik goodbye, wishing he didn't have to leave right away, but he vanished, and she felt a loss like she always did when he was gone, then she joined her father in the house.

He was pacing across the living room and didn't look happy to see her. "While I was dining with some of the king's subjects, I learned what the king had offered you. Why didn't you accept his offer of employment as the princess's lady-in-waiting? You know I barely get by on the retirement the king pays me for being a royal guard to the family for so many years. You were always helping me out. You would have been set for life. You made much better wages while serving as a member of the royal guard, but without that pay—"

"I was going to help you, but I'll work at something." She realized her father hadn't gotten word that the king had offered her old job back too. Would her father prefer that she was still an angel, lost to him? "Nothing is ever set in stone when it comes to king's decrees, you know. What if the king should die? Then everything could change."

"You could have married Cpt. Baldur. Then you wouldn't have to work at all."

"What if the captain displeased the king? Then he could be demoted, and I'd be married to him. What if Princess Esmeralda was sent to another kingdom to wed someone and then if I had been working for her, I would have had to leave you behind?"

"You think it is beneath you to serve as a lady-in-waiting for Princess Esmeralda."

Well, yeah, to an extent. "I wouldn't be able to see Malik, should he come to visit when he could."

Her father threw up his arms in frustration. "Nonsense, Ariana. He is an angel and too busy for a fae. And I'm sure it's forbidden anyway. You should marry the captain."

"I don't love him. I love Malik."

"Love. What do you know about it?"

"I know I can't stop thinking about him. When he's near, he's the only one who is there. Everyone and everything else fades into the background."

"He's a guardian angel. He has a job to do, nothing more. He missed saving your life the first time. He made up for it by bringing you home this time, but that's all there is to it."

"Princess Esmeralda loves Cpt. Baldur. She's the one who should marry him. King Tiernan only wants me to marry the captain so Esmeralda doesn't do it. I thought you'd be more interested in my happiness."

"Longing to be with an angel who can't be with you, who can't support you or take care of you if you're in trouble, even have children with you"—her father shook his head. "You'll tell the king you changed your mind—if not about marrying the captain, then about serving Princess Esmeralda as her lady-in-waiting."

Ariana was beginning to believe returning home had been a mistake. Though if the king hadn't gotten involved in her affairs and her father hadn't been so negative about her relationship with Malik, she wouldn't be grappling with what to do now.

She was saddened to think that her father wasn't happy about the choices she'd made. But she wasn't going to change her mind. She opened the door and stepped out of the cottage.

"Where are you going, Daughter?" her father asked, calling out to her.

"To be with those who will welcome me into their home." Then she strode off. She knew she could stay at any of the castles that the dragons owned. And she could work for them. They didn't stay here often, but they always had a staff on hand, taking care of the castles in their absence.

Her father didn't say anything, but finally shut the door. She knew her father well. He would believe she'd change her mind because he wanted her to. But she wouldn't. He should know her well enough by now also.

She headed for Halloran's castle first. She considered seeing

Brett and Ena, but they might be busy with mated bliss. Hopefully, Halloran wouldn't mind her staying with him.

When she finally reached Halloran's castle, she knocked on the massive doors. A servant answered it and bowed his head.

"I wish to speak with Halloran." She heard laughter inside and it sounded like he was having a party with his friends Olaf, Kiernan, and Amerand.

"Right away." Then the man left and returned quickly with Halloran.

Halloran had been drinking, looking like he was enjoying himself with his dragon friends.

"I'm in need of a place to stay tonight," she said, "if it's not too much trouble."

Raising his brows, Halloran smiled.

Olaf laughed. "Maybe you have a hawk fae, former angel girlfriend now, eh, Halloran?"

"I have an angel to look after me." She smiled at Olaf. "I just need to stay someplace for the night. I would have gone to see Ena and Brett but—"

"They are busy," Halloran said. "I can vouch for that. You and your father—"

"Are at an impasse. He wasn't happy that I didn't take the king up on his offer of employment to serve Princess Esmeralda or to marry the griffin fae captain."

"Ahh. Well, would you care to join us for some honeyed mead?" Halloran motioned to the dining hall.

She hesitated, then agreed. "If Malik returns, do you mind if he stays here with me?"

"Not at all."

The problem would be in getting word to him that she wasn't at her father's cottage, but instead at Halloran's castle. Then she realized he would know it anyway once he saw her dust trail leaving her father's own home and ending up at Halloran's castle.

"Sure, I'll have some mead." Then she followed the dragon fae into the dining hall and she took a seat at the long table. One of his servants poured her a mug of mead. "You don't happen to have a job for me, do you? I seem to need one and a place to stay."

Halloran winked at her.

"He needs a mate," Olaf said.

"Don't listen to him. So does Olaf. But yeah, I need another guard for my staff while I'm not here. You're free to come and go as you please, should Malik come to visit," Halloran said.

She figured Halloran only said that because he really didn't need another guard here.

"The pay is good. Dragons always pay well," he said.

She smiled. "Sure, I'll take the job, thanks." She felt better already and began drinking her mead.

Olaf raised his mug to Halloran. "I didn't know you were such a softy."

"Hey, I'm the one who's fortunate enough to be able to employ a former royal guard who has saved the royal family a number of times. And she can even protect *me* if I need protection."

"Yeah, we see something new about you all the time," Kiernan said.

She smiled at Halloran. She didn't think he'd be someone who would ever need her protection, but the other hawk fae on the staff that weren't trained to fight, sure.

"She can protect *me* when I'm visiting you," Olaf said.

"Me too," Kiernan said.

Amerand agreed also.

She laughed. "I would be honored to."

"Ena's going to be mad that you didn't go to work for her." Halloran took another swig of his mead.

Oh, she hadn't thought of that.

"So if my sister gives me too much trouble over it, she might be hiring you instead. But one of us for sure will have you working for us, and you'll be staying at one of our castles," Halloran said.

"Or you can work for me," Olaf said and Kiernan and Amerand also agreed she could stay at their castles.

She was so glad she had made friends with all of them when they had first come to build their castles here. And if her father needed her help, she could still go over to assist him with the farm and animals. She hoped her father would be fine with the arrangement.

"Believe me, you'll make more than you made as a royal guard for the king," Halloran said.

Her mouth dropped open. "O—kay. That's good news." Her father couldn't fault her for that.

Then she heard a knock at the door. She was hoping Malik had found her fae dust trail and followed it here. That would be just perfect timing.

Before she went to the door to answer it herself as if she lived there, though she guessed she would be from now on, one of Halloran's staff did.

"Uh, aye, she is here, sir."

She hurried out of the dining hall to greet Malik when she saw her father, which totally surprised her. She really had thought it would be Malik. "Dad."

"Hey, I'm sorry. Yeah, I should have your interests at heart. I don't even know why I said what I did," her father said.

Halloran said, "The two of you are welcome to sit in the library and talk."

"Thank you." She and her father went into the library, and they sat down on a couple of the chairs in there. "It's okay, Dad."

"I want you to come home. You're welcome to stay with me. We'll get by just fine."

"I got a job." She smiled. "Halloran hired me to be a guard at his castle. And you know dragons pay better than kings often."

Her father closed his gaping mouth.

"I'll be staying here. If Malik comes looking for me, just tell him I'm living here now and have a job on Halloran's staff. But, Dad, if you need any help at all, don't hesitate to ask for it."

"Are you sure you're all right with this?"

"Oh, better than all right. I'm thrilled. And I'm free to have time to spend with Malik when he shows up."

Her father smiled then. "Okay, I'm happy for you. But if the circumstances ever change for you, you're welcome back home."

"You're not worried the king will be angry with you for my actions, are you?"

"No. I was just concerned no one else would hire you to do a job because of it, afraid the king would be irritated with them. But also, knowing you, you wouldn't be satisfied with sitting at home with me, just taking care of the animals when they needed to be taken to the pastureland."

"Okay, thanks, Dad. Do you want to have some mead with us? We were just having a drink before bed."

"Yeah, I'd like that. Thanks." Then he frowned at her. "You didn't tell me about Claude."

She sighed. "I had to tell the royal family first, and then I just didn't have a chance to tell you." In truth she hadn't wanted to tell her father and then he'd be even madder at her for not even taking her former job back.

"Rex came by the house, said he was a dark fae assassin and told me the whole story. He said for his telling King Tiernan about the plot, you were returning his crimson bow to him."

"I am." She'd actually forgotten that part, so swept up in all this other business.

"He's staying with the royal family since he is a dark fae and the queen is, and she wished to hear more about her home since she has been gone. I'll have a messenger come for the bow and return it to him."

"It's my duty. As soon as we're done here, I'll give it to Rex." She figured her father would want to talk to Halloran a bit, to make sure everything was on the up and up. She truly loved her father.

Then they walked into the dining hall, and he joined them for a drink. He began to speak to Halloran once he had a mug in hand. "So you're hiring my daughter to work for you. What is the arrangement exactly?"

Halloran nodded. "She will be an additional guard and free to help you or take care of her own business whenever she needs to. I'm not here that often, and we're relatively safe, but I do have my gold here and so I do have guards for that reason, and for watching out for the rest of my staff that don't have any fighting skills."

"Okay, that sounds good. And her pay?"

"Dad!" She couldn't believe her father would ask Halloran how much he was going to pay her. That wasn't his business. She'd already told her father that he was paying her more than the king had. That was more than enough.

"Better than what she was paid as a royal guard. I will make sure she is well paid," Halloran said.

The dragons hoarded their gold, but they were known for their generosity when it came to paying their staff members.

"All right. And you have no other interest in my daughter, correct?"

Olaf nearly choked on his mead and started to laugh. Halloran was smiling, good natured about it. Their other friends were chuckling.

"She cares deeply for a guardian angel. Malik has her heart and I have no interest in trying to break up the two. What if I need a guardian angel in the future? I sure wouldn't want to hurt my chances of having one come to my aid. Besides, if I find a fae I want to date, I want her to reciprocate the affection."

Embarrassed, Ariana wanted to melt into the floor, wishing she hadn't invited her father to drink with them, but she realized he had to ask the questions for his own peace of mind.

"All right," her father said. Then he leaned over and gave Ariana a kiss on the cheek. "You take care and if you ever need anything from me, just let me know."

"I'll be visiting, having meals with you whenever you want." Then she walked her father to the door.

"I'm glad we got that all ironed out."

She hugged him. "Just remember to send Malik my way if he shows up. He might be tapping at my window so I'll let him in."

Her father laughed. "Okay. I'll tell him you're at Halloran's castle when he shows up."

And then she returned to the royal castle where Charity, she learned, had the crimson bow in her room for safekeeping in the event the assassin ever had showed up for it. She was just retiring for the night herself and handed Ariana the bow.

"I still can't believe Claude would stoop so low to try and have you killed for your position."

"And then get it in the end anyway!" That was the ironic part about it. He hadn't needed to try and kill Ariana at all. She had killed herself just fine! She took the bow to Rex where he was looking at the view of the stars in the sky from a balcony and he smiled at her. Well, more at the bow in her grasp. "Thank you for all that you've done for me."

"You didn't take your job back," Rex said.

"Truly? I had a better offer."

Rex laughed and took his bow from her and shook her hand. "So did I. And thank you for changing my mind that day. It was well worth it. I never assassinate anyone who doesn't deserve it."

CHAPTER 17

alik couldn't wait to get back to Ariana. Catriona had given him two assignments to deal with. And once he was finished with both, he transported back to the hawk fae kingdom. He tapped at Ariana's window in her father's cottage, then a second time, and a third time. He thought Ariana must be so sound asleep, he couldn't wake her. But then her father came to the window and pulled open the curtains. Uh-oh. He smiled at Malik and motioned for him to come around to the front door.

This couldn't be good.

When Malik reached the door, her father said, "I'd invite you in, but I'm sure you'll want to be with Ariana and she's at Halloran's castle. Just follow her dust trail. She has a job there at a dragon shifter's pay rate and she'll be living there as a guard."

"You are both happy with the arrangement?" Malik asked, thinking there had been a squabble between daughter and father since Ariana had so hastily moved into Halloran's castle.

"We are. I hope you are too. Halloran said he will give her plenty of time to see you. And if she happens to mention it, I told her I had wanted her to marry Cpt. Baldur, but only because she didn't have a job and he could provide for her."

"But she doesn't love him." Malik wanted to make that clear to her father if it wasn't already.

"Aye. But you are an angel."

Which Malik thought he needed to rectify. Now, he needed a way to become one of the fae again because Ariana's dad was right. To truly be with Ariana, Malik needed to be a fae. "That is true. I bid you good night and I'm sure I'll see you again soon."

"Most assuredly." Then her dad closed the door and Malik spread his wings to follow Ariana's dust trail.

He hoped that her dad was right in believing that Malik was welcome at any time at Halloran's castle. Instead of going to the gate, he flew up on top of the wall walk and met a guard.

"You are not here to save me, I take it," the man said.

Malik smiled. "I'm here to see Ariana."

"Halloran said that should you arrive, you are free to join her. She's in the eastern tower, third floor. Halloran put her in that chamber so that you are free to just land on her balcony and knock on the door."

"Thank you." Then Malik flew to the balcony that the guard had motioned to and landed up there. He knocked on the door. He heard rustling and then Ariana's feet hit the floor and she was running to let him in. As soon as she opened the door, he lifted her into his arms, closed the door, and carried her back to bed. "My next mission is to find a way to join you. Permanently."

"So you did know how to become a fae." She snuggled against him in bed.

"I have heard that two had done so, but I don't know how they did it. You know how it is. One minute, they're an angel, the next, like you, a fae again. I haven't seen either of them since then to know how they did it."

"Oh, sure, and we still don't even know how it happened to me, so it's possible they won't have a clue either."

He let out his breath. "Yeah, you're right."

"Okay, so if you're supposed to save someone and you die while rescuing them, then become an angel, what exactly happened to you?" Ariana asked Malik again.

He sighed. "I managed to help the men right their boat after several attempts. Neither could get into the boat on their own. I transported the first man into the boat and once he was safely aboard, we tried to pull the other man into the boat, but we couldn't manage. I dove into the water and boosted the second man into the boat. I had planned to help them get to shore, but before I could transport into the boat, or just climb aboard, the boat crashed into me, hitting me hard on the head."

"Knocking you out."

"Not quite. Before I lost consciousness or could transport, a shark bit me."

Ariana's jaw dropped. "You were eaten by a shark! You said that before, but I assumed you were jesting."

"Nobody believed it. That's why it took me a day longer than you to recover from my injuries and be whole again."

"Ohmigoddess, you poor thing."

"That was part of why I was so angry with Elwin for putting you in the turbulent sea filled with sharks during a thunderstorm. I could just envision myself being there, pre-angel business."

"I can imagine."

"But your situation was by far worse what with the raging storm and dealing with four sharks."

"Yeah, but I was an angel so at least I couldn't die. Well, I kept hoping I couldn't."

* * *

EARLY THE NEXT MORNING, Brett banged at Halloran's door while Malik and Ariana were breaking their fast with Halloran and his staff. The butler showed Brett into the great hall. Brett hurried to say, "Eleron has located Faraday. Well, we both did. Together. We're able to break through his spell that cloaks his castle. It's located near the winged fae realm. I'm sure they have no idea it is even there."

Halloran immediately rose from the high table. "I'm ready to go."

"We still don't know how powerful he is. Are you sure you want to pursue this?" Brett asked. "No doubt only magic users will have any success at defeating him."

Ena suddenly entered the great hall with Sigrid, queen of the falcon fae in tow. "Sigrid has come to help us."

"So that means three mages against one wizard," Malik said, hoping that would be enough.

"And an angel for additional protection," Halloran said.

"I'm going too," Ariana said.

Malik suspected she wouldn't want to be left behind, though he preferred she'd stay at Halloran's castle.

"Sinbad, king of the griffin fae, is coming also," Ena said. "Since the griffin had made a pact with King Tiernan now, and Tiernan is sending his own mage to deal with this, Sinbad wants to help us as well."

"Good. Then if the rest of us dragons are needed, we'll be there for you," Halloran told the mages.

It was decided then that the four mages would be enough to take down Faraday, no matter what abilities he had.

Malik just hoped he wouldn't get called away in the middle of all this action. He took Halloran aside as everyone prepared to leave. Ariana was returning to her chamber to dress in her leather armor. "If I'm called away, can you watch out for Ariana? I know you're paying her to guard you, but—"

Halloran slapped him on the back. "Don't give it another thought. I'll see that she remains safe."

That's all Malik needed was to lose Ariana for good. He didn't think Catriona would welcome her back to the angel realm if she should die again.

Then the dragons gathered in Halloran's courtyard, the mages too, an angel, and one stubborn hawk fae, whom Malik loved dearly.

He was still surprised King Sinbad would leave his kingdom to join in the battle, though since the griffin fae had stopped warring with the hawk fae, he figured fighting was just in his blood. Malik was also surprised Sigrid's mage king mate, Owen, wouldn't be with her, but they'd just taken over the kingdom, so Malik assumed they were still concerned about the split in the falcon fae kingdom. Two separate kingdoms ruled their own dominions, so someone had to stay home and keep the status quo, since the brother and sister, Sigrid's cousins, ruling the other kingdom were also magic users.

"What did you say to Halloran while I was gone?" Ariana asked, armed with a bow and quiver of arrows as Malik flew her in the direction of the winged fae kingdom.

"That he is to keep you safe, should Catriona call me away."

"Thank you."

Malik hadn't expected her to thank him for it. "You're welcome." He didn't say any more than that to her, knowing that's all that needed to be said, and he was glad she hadn't been perturbed with him.

They finally reached Faraday's castle at the edge of a forest and Malik worried that the wizard had made it visible just for them to see it and then he'd entrap them with his magic, like he'd done to Ariana. Though according to her, he hadn't realized he could trap an angel there using his magic.

The castle appeared empty—no guards on the wall walk. The dragons alighted up there first, followed by the mages. There was no one in the courtyard either. But when Malik set Ariana down on the wall walk, she pointed to a tower window.

A blue flash of light shot out from the tower, and everyone

scattered to avoid being hit. The bolt of blue light struck trees in the distance and froze them solid.

"He's a winter mage," Brett warned from the top of another tower where he, Ena, Malik and Ariana had settled next.

Sigrid soon joined them. "Maybe I could send him to the unseelie world." She had done that before with a powerful mage and griffin fae warriors. Who knew what had become of them? But opening a portal between the seelie and unseelie planes of existence could be dangerous. If the unseelie broke through, the seelie and unseelie could have a real war on their hands.

"You notice he didn't hit the wall walk with his freezing spell," Ariana said. "He was trying to preserve his castle, aiming at us, but we scattered too quickly."

"I'll try and blow him out of the tower," Brett said, and he cast a whirlwind spell at the tower, slamming into it, sending a desk and books flying out through another window and dropping them to the forest floor.

"He probably moved to another location," Malik said, "knowing we'd retaliate."

"We'll need to go inside and find him," Sinbad said, joining them on top of the tower.

"Wait, what is that off in the distance? A light as bright as the sun," Ariana said.

"My grandfather," Brett said, smiling. "Sol, the sun dragon."

They waited for the dragon to grow closer, Malik not believing a dragon could glow so brightly in the sun's rays that he looked as though he could outshine the sun.

"He's also a magic user," Brett explained. "And it appears he learned we were involved in this adventure and wanted to help out."

Brett waved to Sol from atop the tower and Sol headed straight for it, his scales merely a shiny gold now, not like the blinding sun.

"Faraday is a winter mage," Brett warned him as Sol landed on the rooftop.

"Good," Sol said. "Then you will find a sun mage a useful addition to your forces." He glanced at Malik. "Who are you protecting?"

"Ariana and anyone else who needs protecting," Malik said.

Sol looked Ariana over. "You are not a mage, nor a dragon."

"I'm Halloran's guard," Ariana said, her chin tilted up.

Sol smiled. "He is lucky to have you. Are we ready to take care of this dark magic user?"

"Aye," Malik said, before anyone else could respond. He wanted to finish this before he had to leave to do an angel mission and he would then be worrying about Ariana's safety.

They all broke up into teams and left for the other towers, but Ena, Brett, and Halloran stayed with Malik and Ariana. They heard a blasting noise down below as they checked all the tower rooms on the way down the stairs but found no one in any of the rooms. Once they reached the bottom of the stairs, they rushed into the great hall. There they saw Kiernan and Olaf frozen solid as dragons.

"I can't unfreeze them," Brett said.

But Ena was still in her dragon form, and she blasted first Olaf, then Kiernan with fire, surprising Malik. Ariana seemed to realize what was going on already.

He shouldn't have been surprised, he realized. The dragon's scales were impervious to fire. They couldn't be harmed in that way. Both dragons quickly thawed out.

"What happened here?" Brett asked.

Kiernan turned into his fae form to talk. "We saw him, and we both flamed him with dragon fire, but he triggered balls of ice to come out of cannons in the walls at us. Once we were frozen, the balls stopped shooting out of the walls."

"But he triggered them, not you?" Brett asked, and Malik

knew he was trying to ascertain if the wizard had been here at the same time.

"Aye, he did."

Then they heard a dragon's cry in another tower—the one to the northeast of their location.

"Amerand," Brett said, already turning into his dragon and headed that way with the other dragons.

But Malik knew Ariana would be in trouble if the wizard froze her. If a mage could safely unfreeze her, that was one thing. But if not, she could be dead. As an angel, hopefully, he couldn't be hurt. He hoped he wouldn't anger her—too much—but he couldn't risk her life and he felt he had no other choice at this point. Either he would have to leave her with the winged fae, and he didn't even know if they would give her safe haven or not, or he could return her to the angel realm, which wasn't allowed. One or the other, and he chose the place where he felt she would be the safest.

He grabbed her up in his arms, startling her, and transported her to his chamber in the angel realm and kissed her. "I'll be back for you soon."

"Oh, no, Malik. You did not just return me to the angel realm."

"To keep you safe. I will return." Then Malik left before Ariana made him change his mind, though he guessed he should have told her to stay put in his chamber and not venture out of the room. But he figured she'd realize she needed to.

When he returned to Faraday's castle and was standing on the castle ramparts, he saw Sigrid shooting blasts of lightning at Faraday. Brett was fortifying her effort. Sinbad was shielding them from anything the winter wizard threw at them—daggers of ice, freezing spells, balls of ice—while Halloran gathered the dragons at Faraday's back and with their inborn flame throwers, they hit him with everything they had.

"Where is my guardian angel when I need one?" Faraday

shouted to Malik as the wizard fought to protect himself from the fire and electricity slamming into his defenses.

"You're not on any to-save list, not after you planned to keep an angel for your own," Malik called out.

Sol suddenly whipped around the wizard and directed the sunlight to reflect off his scales into the wizard's eyes, momentarily blinding the winter wizard. Faraday's defenses dropped, his concentration lost and one of the bolts of lightning Sigrid let loose penetrated his magic defensive shield and his heart, stopping him cold. Faraday dropped to the ground dead.

He had been a powerful wizard. One who could fight several forces at once and still continue to assault them. In the end, his isolationism and arrogance, and the wrong he had done by protecting Duke Tully's illegal activities had brought about his downfall.

Malik was glad they had resolution in this, and he was eager to return to his chamber to bring Ariana home, but he had to congratulate everyone for a job well done first.

Ena joined him and shifted into her fae. "Where's Ariana? I was worried about her."

"In the angel realm for safekeeping."

"Oh. Good." Then Ena frowned. "Can you do that? Take a fae there?"

"I didn't know anyone in the winged fae kingdom, the closest to where Faraday's castle was. I didn't want to chance leaving her there."

"All right. I understand. We're celebrating at King Tiernan's castle. But after that, we're returning to our respective kingdoms," Ena said.

"I'll bring Ariana there," Malik said.

Ena smiled. "She couldn't have a better dragon than my brother to work for. Well, except for me."

Malik laughed.

Then everyone headed back to the hawk fae kingdom—dragons, a falcon, and a griffin, while Malik tried to return to the angel realm. He realized then he had no angel wings and his phantom fae aura was showing. No! He couldn't be stuck here while Ariana was stranded in his chamber at the angel realm.

Had Catriona returned him to the fae world for good for taking a fae to the angel realm? Just like Ariana had done with Duke Tully? What if Catriona decided to turn Ariana back into an angel and leave Malik trapped in the fae world? Though he didn't believe she could do that with a fae without her dying first.

He just stood there, staring up at the heavens above, as if he'd suddenly see Ariana dropping down out of the clouds and into his arms as soon as she was discovered there. He couldn't believe his mistake in not just taking her to the winged fae kingdom.

"Ariana!" he shouted into the wind, as if he could reach her that way, and he swore he heard her sigh.

CHAPTER 18

*A*riana had waited for Malik to return for her for so long, she'd actually fallen asleep on his bed when the door opened and a light from the hallway spilled into the dark room. She sat up in bed, thinking it was Malik, but the blond haired, male fae smiling at her was not any fae she'd ever seen before.

"Either Catriona mixed up room assignments or she's giving out fae girlfriends to newly promoted first class angels. So who might you be?"

"Where...where's Malik?" Ariana hurried out of bed, worried Malik had gotten himself killed, but how could he?

"Rumors abound he's not returning here, which is why I have his chamber now."

Ariana hurriedly brushed past the angel and headed down the hall to Juno's chamber. Once she arrived there, she didn't even knock on her door she was so rattled. She opened it and barged into the room, but then saw the bed was empty. Then she heard laughter down the hall and recognized both Elwin and Juno's voices. Ariana quickly left Juno's room and both of them stopped dead in their tracks and they just stared at her with incredulity.

"What are you doing here?" Juno asked, running to join Ariana. Elwin hurried to catch up to her.

"Malik brought me here for my own protection. Mages and dragons were fighting Faraday, a winter wizard, and Malik was afraid Faraday would kill me, so he brought me to his chamber. Where is he?"

Elwin and Juno exchanged looks.

"We've got to get you home now." Juno looked at Elwin as if to see if he agreed.

He held his hands up, saying whatever they did was fine with him. Then Juno took Ariana's hand, but Elwin gathered Ariana into his arms, and they returned to the hawk fae kingdom.

They heard a celebration going on at the royal family's castle and they headed that way. When they entered the castle, Ariana couldn't believe Malik would join the others here and forget all about her! But she didn't see any sign of him.

Ena hurried over to join her and the angels. "Where's Malik?" she asked as if Ariana should know!

"He left me at the angel realm. Elwin and Juno had to return me here. Where did you see Malik last?"

"Faraday's castle. He said he was going to get you and bring you here," Ena said.

"What if the castle had more booby traps and Malik's frozen there? I'll be back." At least now Ariana could transport herself there since Faraday's castle wasn't too far to transport to. She couldn't believe Malik would stay at Faraday's castle for any good reason when everyone else appeared to be partying at King Tiernan's castle and that had her worried.

But when she reached Faraday's castle, there Malik was. Standing atop a castle tower, looking up at the sky, and he wasn't wearing wings, but his phantom fae aura cloaked him instead! Ohmigod. He was now a fae like her?

She smiled. "Malik!"

He turned his head to see her standing on the wall walk and

transported to her before she could reach his location. He took her into his arms and hugged the breath from her.

Both Elwin and Juno had followed her dust trail and joined them.

Ena and Brett came too in case Malik had been in trouble.

"Ohmigoddess, Malik. You're no longer one of us," Juno exclaimed.

Ariana couldn't believe it. Tears filled her eyes. She hugged Malik tight and kissed him like there was no tomorrow. She hoped he was all right with being just one of the fae again, but she was worried he would miss being one of the angels.

"Nah," Elwin said, folding his arms and smiling. "I'm afraid Malik and Ariana will always be one of our kind. And it appears Malik is just as special as Ariana."

"You bet he is," Ariana said.

"Let's join the party before some of us have to get back to work," Elwin said.

"What will you do now?" Juno asked Malik.

"Do you think Halloran will need another guard on his staff?" Malik asked.

"I wouldn't doubt it," Ariana said.

"But if he doesn't, you can both work and live with Brett and me at our castle," Ena said.

And then the six of them went to the hawk fae kingdom and partied until Juno and Elwin were called away.

Halloran was all too happy to give Malik a position as a guard also since he'd been a royal guard for the phantom fae.

Best of all, Ariana's father welcomed Malik into the family for good, with talk of wanting grandchildren with all haste.

This time when Ariana retired to her chamber with Malik, he was no longer an angel, but just another fae and both of them were overjoyed for it.

* * *

"I WONDER what will happen to Duke Tully," Ariana said the next morning as they broke their fast with Halloran and the other dragons before the dragon fae returned to the dragon kingdom.

"Once his island was revealed, he'd have the devil to pay," Halloran said, grabbing one last jellied scone. Then he smiled. "And no angel to save him this time."

Then the dragons left, and Malik and Ariana began training some of the staff in defensive tactics just in case they ever needed them, since they weren't really busy guarding anything.

They were using staffs and parrying with some of the cooks and maids when two of the men looked up at the wall walk and everyone glanced in that direction to see what had caught their eye.

Four angels were sitting atop the wall walk watching them, then flew down to meet with them.

"So what makes you so special?" a redheaded male angel asked Malik and Ariana.

"How did you return to the fae world?" a dark-haired female angel asked.

A male whose hair was just as dark said, "Some say you were never angels. That it was all just a hoax."

Malik and Ariana smiled at his comment.

A blond male frowned at them. "How did you die?"

"Malik was eaten by a shark. Surely even you have heard his story. Have you watched the angel training videos? My favorite one is of him setting the brakes on a stroller so the young girl couldn't push it into the street."

Malik wrapped his arm around Ariana. "Ariana is the one who is truly special and loving her made me special too. If you haven't seen it, you can watch the harrowing encounter Ariana had with four sharks while rescuing a paddler in a raging storm. But don't take my word for it. Elwin can tell you all about it."

The blond looked at the other angels. "I've got an assignment."

"Me too," the girl said.

Both of them vanished.

"Elwin, eh?" Then the dark-haired, male angel left.

"No, really, how did you do it? Return to the fae world?" the redhead asked.

"We haven't a clue," Ariana said.

Malik agreed.

But the redhead frowned. "I will learn the truth." Then he vanished.

"See, Malik, that's just what I said," Ariana said.

Malik laughed. "Yeah, I knew you were trouble the moment I laid eyes on you."

"And worth it, right?"

"Oh, aye."

Then they went back to training and loving every minute of it and loving each other too.

EPILOGUE

King Tiernan might not have been totally happy that Ariana had turned him down for not one but three of his proposals, but Queen Ritasia and Princess Esmeralda put on a wedding for Malik and Ariana that was suitable for royalty. All the dragon fae they knew also attended. Even Queen Irenis of the dark fae came to see her daughter, Ritasia, and to be at the wedding and join in on the celebration. It wasn't often that the fae attended a wedding of two former guardian angels.

But even more fun, Elwin and Juno came to their wedding and even Catriona made a very brief and unexpected appearance. But once she left, six more angels arrived at the festivities.

Ariana's father couldn't have been more delighted to give his daughter away to Malik. Charity, Juno, Esmeralda, Ena, and Xalta were thrilled to be matrons of honor and bridesmaids. Elwin, Halloran, Brett, and the other dragons served as Malik's groomsmen, Brett being his best man.

And even King Tiernan raised a toast to the couple and said, "To a match made in heaven and here in the fae realm."

"Here! here!"

As to King Tully? He was in hiding, no one knew where. And

his people were now running the castle on Mystic Island and fishing in the sea for a living. Before Sigrid left for her kingdom, she had sent Claude to the unseelie plane. Not a good place for any seelie to be and there was no coming back for him.

Ariana even saw Esmeralda dancing a couple of times with Cpt. Baldur. Maybe the king would eventually change his mind about her marrying him. He was the tyrant king after all, from a long line of tyrant kings, though he'd vowed once he had become king, he'd never be like the rest of his family. Ritasia had helped to see that he wasn't. Most of the time.

"I was thinking of our honeymoon," Malik said to Ariana, as he danced with her again.

"You know there's only one place we can go for it."

Some fae liked the human convention of having a honeymoon after marrying a fae. And she and Malik had both wanted it.

"South Padre Island," they both said at the same time.

Queen Irenis overheard them and said, "We will make sure you are undisturbed."

They both smiled at her. That was just what they both wanted to hear.

They wouldn't need bags when they went. They'd pick up whatever they needed—in the fae way.

They'd get the honeymoon suite where they wanted to, free meals at the best restaurants, clothes at their favorite boutiques. Whatever they wanted. And wouldn't pay a dime for it—courtesy of being able to control human minds.

The party was still going when the two of them slipped away to be together on South Padre Island. When they arrived on the beach, they took in the sea breeze that blew their hair about and they held each other's hands.

They were watching swimmers out on a sandbar, the deep trough between that and the shallow water near shore. Ariana could see a riptide current, and she kept an eye on the swimmer crossing it when suddenly Juno and Elwin were there standing beside them.

"Catriona said you're to play with each other, not rescue anyone at the beach—today. That's our job. Go. Have. Fun," Juno said.

Elwin smiled. "That's what she told us."

Then the dark fae showed up in royal guard uniforms. They were only visible to the fae and the angels. Not the humans.

"We're here to ensure you are undisturbed," one of the dark fae guards said.

Now that was a new one for the books. Malik and Ariana would have their own royal guards for the time-being.

"We have some business to take care of then," Malik said and with a nod to his angel friends and the royal guards, he took Ariana to the nicest hotel they could find and talked the hotel clerk into giving them a newlywed suite for a week. Of course, he persuaded the clerk with his innate fae ability that one of them was theirs and they'd even paid for it.

And then with the keycard in hand, he took Ariana to the honeymoon suite.

"I love you, Malik."

"You will always be the only one for me," Malik said, carrying her over the threshold and letting the door slam closed behind him. "From the first time I saw you." And boy, he had to go through heaven and earth to make it all work out. "I love you."

ACKNOWLEDGMENTS

Thanks so much to my voracious readers, Darla Taylor and Donna Fournier, who are busily getting ready for Thanksgiving! Happy holidays and many, many thanks for reading my stories first to make them the best they can be!

ABOUT THE AUTHOR

USA Today bestselling and award-winning author **Terry Spear** has written over a hundred paranormal romance novels, young adult, and medieval Highland historical romances. Her first werewolf romance, *Heart of the Wolf,* was named a 2008 *Publishers Weekly*'s Best Book of the Year, and her subsequent titles have garnered high praise and hit the *USA Today* bestseller list. A retired officer of the U.S. Army Reserves, Terry lives in Spring, Texas, where she is working on her next werewolf romance, shapeshifting jaguars, cougar shifters, vampires, hot Highlanders, and having fun with her young adult novels, helping with her granddaughter and grandson and raising two havanese.

For more information, please visit her website at: http://www.terryspear.com

Blog: https://terryspearbooks.blog/

Follow her for new releases and book deals: www.bookbub.com/authors/terry-spear

Twitter: @TerrySpear.

Facebook: http://www.facebook.com/terry.spear

ALSO BY TERRY SPEAR

Wild Highland Lass (novella), Vexing the Highlander (novella), My Highlander

Other historical romances: Lady Caroline & the Egotistical Earl, A Ghost of a Chance at Love

* * *

Heart of the Wolf Series: Heart of the Wolf, Destiny of the Wolf, To Tempt the Wolf, Legend of the White Wolf, Seduced by the Wolf, Wolf Fever, Heart of the Highland Wolf, Dreaming of the Wolf, A SEAL in Wolf's Clothing, A Howl for a Highlander, A Highland Werewolf Wedding, A SEAL Wolf Christmas, Silence of the Wolf, Hero of a Highland Wolf, A Highland Wolf Christmas, A SEAL Wolf Hunting; A Silver Wolf Christmas, A SEAL Wolf in Too Deep, Alpha Wolf Need Not Apply, Billionaire in Wolf's Clothing, Between a Rock and a Hard Place, SEAL Wolf Undercover, Dreaming of a White Wolf Christmas, Flight of the White Wolf, All's Fair in Love and Wolf, A Billionaire Wolf for Christmas, SEAL Wolf Surrender (2019), Silver Town Wolf: Home for the Holidays (2019), Wolff Brothers: You Had Me at Wolf, Night of the Billionaire Wolf, Joy to the Wolves (Red Wolf), The Wolf Wore Plaid, Jingle Bell Wolf, Best of Both Wolves, While the Wolf's Away

SEAL Wolves: To Tempt the Wolf, A SEAL in Wolf's Clothing, A SEAL Wolf Christmas, A SEAL Wolf Hunting, A SEAL Wolf in Too Deep, SEAL Wolf Undercover, SEAL Wolf Surrender (2019)

Silver Bros Wolves: Destiny of the Wolf, Wolf Fever, Dreaming of the Wolf, Silence of the Wolf, A Silver Wolf Christmas, Alpha Wolf Need Not Apply, Between a Rock and a Hard Place, All's Fair in Love and Wolf, Silver Town Wolf: Home for the Holidays (2019)

Wolff Brothers of Silver Town

Billionaire Wolves: Billionaire in Wolf's Clothing, A Billionaire Wolf for Christmas, Night of the Billionaire Wolf

Highland Wolves: Heart of the Highland Wolf, A Howl for a Highlander, A Highland Werewolf Wedding, Hero of a Highland Wolf, A Highland Wolf Christmas, Wolf Wore Plaid

Red Wolf Series: Seduced by the Wolf, Joy to the Wolves

* * *

Heart of the Jaguar Series: Savage Hunger, Jaguar Fever, Jaguar Hunt, Jaguar Pride, A Very Jaguar Christmas, You Had Me at Jaguar)

Novella: The Witch and the Jaguar

Dawn of the Jaguar

* * *

Romantic Suspense: Deadly Fortunes, In the Dead of the Night, Relative Danger, Bound by Danger

* * *

Vampire romances: Killing the Bloodlust, Deadly Liaisons, Huntress for Hire, Forbidden Love, Vampire Redemption, Primal Desire

Vampire Novellas: Vampiric Calling, The Siren's Lure, Seducing the Huntress

* * *

Other Romance: Exchanging Grooms, Marriage, Las Vegas Style

* * *

Science Fiction Romance: Galaxy Warrior

Teen/Young Adult/Fantasy Books

The World of Fae:

The Dark Fae, Book 1

The Deadly Fae, Book 2

The Winged Fae, Book 3

The Ancient Fae, Book 4

Dragon Fae, Book 5

Hawk Fae, Book 6

Phantom Fae, Book 7

Golden Fae, Book 8

Falcon Fae, Book 9

Woodland Fae, Book 10

Angel Fae, Book 11

The World of Elf:

The Shadow Elf

Darkland Elf

Blood Moon Series:

Kiss of the Vampire

The Vampire…In My Dreams

Demon Guardian Series:

The Trouble with Demons

Demon Trouble, Too

Demon Hunter

Non-Series for Now:

Ghostly Liaisons

The Beast Within

Courtly Masquerade

Deidre's Secret

The Magic of Inherian:

The Scepter of Salvation

The Mage of Monrovia

Emerald Isle of Mists (TBA)